About the author

The Very Raving Mr P is an author of reality-based fantasy fiction, and an amateur politician for the Official Monster Raving Loony Party.

He chooses to spend his time on this mortal coil writing stories about alien dwarves, mysterious murders, and time travellers, while also attempting to discuss real life physics and phenomena.

Unlike the characters in his stories, he is scared of heights, confined spaces, and anything slightly dangerous. In truth he would never be the hero in his own stories.

And so he writes…

THE MEANING OF LIFE

THE VERY RAVING MR P

THE MEANING OF LIFE

Vanguard Press

A CIP catalogue record for this title is
available from the British Library.

ISBN 978 1 80016 310 2

*Vanguard Press is an imprint of
Pegasus Elliot MacKenzie Publishers Ltd.*
www.pegasuspublishers.com

First Published in 2022

**Vanguard Press
Sheraton House Castle Park
Cambridge England**

Printed & Bound in Great Britain

Dedication

To all the Loonies and Geeks on planet Earth

The Meaning of Life

There have been five mass extinctions on planet Earth in its 4.55 billion years of existence.

Five mass extinctions, and one mass exodus.

The one mass exodus took place during the time that an intelligent, erect postured, bipedal primate, called humans occupied the Earth.

Now, humans were a blessed species, being as they were, beneficiaries of a consequence of evolution that favoured complex language, binocular vision, and high dexterity due to having opposable thumbs. But ultimately, they suffered from being a bit jittery.

There had been evidence, on many occasions, where humans were prone to bouts of unpredictability and irrational thought processes, but of which, for the most part, made them a lovable species that had been extensively studied by other life forms higher up in the food chain.

The unfortunate exodus in question happened after an administrative error by an office clerk, called Debbie, who was working her first shift at the World Health Organisation on a bright and sunny Monday afternoon. Well, I say an administrative error, it was more like an auto correct error, but let's not get bogged down with inconsequential details.

But the thing was this, one of Debbie's first tasks in her new job was to document the minutes of an emergency climate change meeting. The gathering was the usual nonsense of droll rhetoric from boring world leaders who are temporary custodians of importance. And all was going well, until a particularly excitable activist stood up and shouted, 'We need to love our planet as of tomorrow or we will all die.'

Now that all seems innocent enough you might say, and indeed that is what Debbie intended to write down. But unfortunately, her laptop auto corrected the word "love" to "leave", and as humans were prone to irrational bouts of panicking, they are a jittery bunch as I've already said, by lunch the following day, all human inhabitants of planet Earth had found transport to Proxima Centauri b, and left.

Thus, the Earth is now dominated by life forms called Dinglewits that were visiting Earth from their home planet of "Luyten b".

The irony of the tale is that the Dinglewits had visited Proxima Centauri b, now occupied by humans, while on route to Earth and noted in their ships log: 'Proxima Centauri b is a dump — do not go there.'

The Dinglewits and the Earthlings never met. They passed each other while navigating the rings around Uranus, but did not exchange words due to it being semi-final day at Wimbledon.

Debbie slept-in that morning and missed her transport.

Now unlike the humans, Dinglewits are an unimaginative bunch. It had been many centuries since they had bothered to invent anything new, or create a piece of artwork, or write a barnstorming novel. No indeed, Dinglewits much preferred to copy other lifeforms' lifestyles rather than think of their own, and adopt other species' mannerisms, rather than be interesting enough to have their own. In fact, the Dinglewit species are described as being as dull as dishwater in the universal encyclopaedia cosmopolital. And many think that that was a complimentary remark. And so, in true Dinglewit fashion they occupied earth, adopted human cultures, watched all their TV shows, listened to their music, learned to speak their language, and behaved pretty much in a similar way.

In truth, the Earth carried on exactly from where the humans left off. Just with Dinglewits on it instead.

And as for Debbie — Well, we'll get to her later.

The conventional insanity of beauty

It is nice to live in interesting times, but if you don't, then make the times you live in interesting. Because to understand the meaning of one's existence is to understand why we are, or indeed, why we aren't. And it takes a special arrangement of neuronal configuration to fully grasp the question, and be willing to die to achieve the answer.

A great philosopher once said, that it is only when confronted by sheer lunacy is clarity of thought truly achieved. But unfortunately, the Dinglewits opted against clarity of thought and instead chose the beautiful world of sheer ignorance.

In this mind-set they were relatively happy. They travelled the universe without a care in the world, enjoying all it had to offer, and basking in the bosoms of its beauty. Until one day, when a curious Dinglewit living on planet Earth had a thought. It was just an ordinary thought. It wasn't a thought that required any particular skill or knowledge. And it probably wasn't a thought that had never been thought of before at some point in the history of the universe. It was just a thought. But nothing would ever be the same again.

That particular Dinglewit was called Mr P. He was not what you would call, handsome looking, in the classical sense of the word, being as he was, a short stout fellow with a ginger beard and no hair, but what he lacked in looks he more than made up for in style.

Always smartly turned-out, he was something of a dandy when it came to fashion. Never would he be seen without a shirt and bow tie, accompanied by a rather groovy pair of shorts, and the latest in footwear.

He lived in G-Town, which is a valley town in the middle lands of Britannia most famous for a rather tasty biscuit made from ginger, and very little else.

So it's not really the obvious setting for the greatest story ever to be written. And you could be forgiven that a story based around an "ordinary" from the most boring town ever may not exactly deliver anything of any real interest — but you are mistaken.

That's because Mr P had a singular irreplaceable thought. A thought so singular and irreplaceable, that it can only be described as a singular and irreplaceable thought.

Now the overlords of the Dinglewits had discouraged thinking of any kind, because they felt that everything of worth had already been thought of, so their time is much better spent enjoying themselves. A noble gesture you might say. But Mr P could not shake this silly question from his head. He knew it would lead to no good, and perhaps even get him into trouble, but nevertheless it was a thought, and to him anyway, it was important.

'Gertie?' said Mr P as they were sitting outside on a patio drinking a particularly potent home brew that had strange sort of lemony taste. 'Have you ever wondered what this is all about?'

Now for those that have never met Mr P, he speaks very well indeed — some might say he sounds quite posh. A trait most rare for a Dinglewit from G-Town.

'All what is about?' Gertie replied. Gertie does not sound posh.

'This… why are we here? What is our purpose?' he continued.

'Do you mean what is the meaning of life?' Gertie answered.

'YES, YES, YES, YES,' came the rather excited response. 'What is the meaning of life?'

'Not really,' Gertie answered. 'I heard that a human once asked that question but the answer was inconclusive.'

'Well, I want to know!' Mr P intervened. 'There must be a reason for all this nonsense, otherwise, what's the point?'

Now in between moments of sexual excellence and home cooking, Gertie was quite the philosopher. She would often pass away her evenings reading the writings of, the human, Confucius or, the Dinglewit, Sarvige. So she knew some stuff.

'We have tried to seek the meaning of life before ya know,' Gertie stated, much to the surprise of Mr P. 'Really? When?'

'Oh, it was some time ago now, it was written in the Great Scriptures of Kasandra.'

The Great Scriptures of Kasandra are writings of historic value that were found in the Sea of Life on the planet LHS 1140 b by the explorer Chowara Terda. A promising young chap, who suddenly just dropped dead on the spot.

Mr P knew of these scriptures from his time at the Revered Order where he read pretty much anything to get out of doing activities. In short, the conclusion was that the meaning of life was the number 42, but this was based on a human book written hundreds of years ago and had never been validated, if anything, thought Mr P, it should have been the number 106, but everyone knows that that isn't true either. But in all honesty, it was all probably just an inverted pyramid of piffle, and that it's probably just some sort of symbol.

'The Great Scriptures of Kasandra are over-rated, babe, Mr P stated, 'they were written in a more ignorant time when no one knew about... well, all the stuff we know about today.'

'All the stuff we know about today!' came the exasperated response, 'spoken like everything we know, is all that there is to know, eh,' Gertie replied.

'Exactly, Gertie. There is still so much to discover. So much knowledge and understanding to be sought.'

He stood up. 'Let's go on an epic adventure!' he shouted with both arms aloft. 'Let us seek out the significance of it all, Gertie, let us discover once and for all whether there is a meaning to life, or whether it's just one big farce,' he said enthusiastically, 'Let us discover… The Meaning of Life.'

'OK,' replied Gertie.

'Really?'

'Yeah, why not! It could be fun.'

'Fun,' thought Mr P. 'Yes it will be fun babe,' he answered, with some hesitancy in his voice.

And he sat back down with a big Cheshire cat grin on his face, and continued with his home brew.

A trip, a badge, and a time machine

A holiday was in order.

Mr P wanted to go hiking, but Gertie suggested Marrakesh, she had always dreamed of going to the old markets and experience the hustle and bustle. So they compromised, and went to Marrakesh.

He didn't mind though, he had heard that the Atlas Mountains are to be visited at least once in every Dinglewits lifetime. He also thought that a trip to a far away and ancient culture would be a good start in his adventure into finding the meaning of life.

And so with great cheerfulness in their hearts, they toddled off to the sunshine. And the great adventure began. The great adventure that would, eventually, lead to the most important discovery in the history of the entire universe.

Well… Sort of…

The weather was hot and the old town of Marrakesh was bustling with energy. There were snake charmers, pickpockets, over-priced pieces of pottery, really bad smells and worse food. All the usual stuff that tourists expected when visiting exotic and far-flung places.

While walking through the inner-city caverns — that are obviously kept old as a tourist trap — Mr P received a message from his ol' friend Aryn — a particularly colourful character who spends much of his time drinking local ales at the Red Lion in his local village.

Now, the mentioning of Aryn doesn't really add anything to this story, but it's just an interesting fact that they both were avid badge collectors. The message read that he had recently acquired Looney Lord Piddlehinton's badge depicting the order of the 2nd Elephant Brigade, and he thought it looked immense. Mr P loved a good badge and would never be seen without one attached to his lapel.

But one thing he did notice while traipsing through the old town caverns was that everyone was walking in the same direction. There seemed to be an unconscious flow to life here, like ants in an ant farm. No one was walking against the flow. And seeing as he was now seeking meaning to all things, it got him thinking. 'Is this logical? Is there a flow to thoughts? Are we merely designed to follow the crowds? Are we herd thinkers? Do we come to a better conclusion when we are in higher numbers? Is that the meaning of life… to be part of a herd? Is herd happiness the answer?'

Mr P had always supposed that happiness was freedom of thought, and the ability to think of something original and act on those thoughts. However, since the guidance from the High Council to discourage uncontrolled thinking was published, Dinglewits tended not to bother with that. You see, the authorities have a big issue with thinking, and with individuals having the ability to think. It is very awkward for them to control you see, and we know what happens when individuals cannot be controlled, don't we? No, it is much more convenient if everyone just did as they were told and left the thinking to them. After all, they are in charge.

'Babe,' called Gertie as she noticed Mr P staring motionless at a wooden phalanx, 'what say we get some food?'

'Food, Gertie, fooood… I can't think of food at a time like this. I was thinking about the freedom of thought, babe, do you believe in destiny?' he replied.

'No, no, no.' Jumped Gertie. 'Look at the problems the Acerimans are having with it! We don't wanna get involved in any of that.'

'Well, I have read a theory that the universe controls everything. Before we are born our lives are planned out, and we just follow a set path that has been pre- determined. Sure, we can change a few minor things, but really our fate is sealed before we are born.'

Mr P and Gertie looked at each other.

'But why would the universe bother to plan out the lives of every living Dinglewit? That is soooo much effort. And for what? What would the universe get from it?'

'I don't know, Gertie. Perhaps control. Yeah, that's it, the universe is a control freak,' he replied.

'But where is the fun in that. Wouldn't the universe be much more intrigued to see what happens if freedom of thought was granted? Where every Dinglewit could decide for themselves! Where every life form could decide for themselves! I think the universe would much rather see that.'

'You could be right, Gertie. But fate has nothing to do with freedom of thought. You see, we can think what we want, but fate is always the natural end of things,' he stated.

'Well, that's what the Acerimans think, but something's happening over there and we ain't getting involved in any of that,' Gertie answered.

Mr P knew she was right. Gertie was normally right. He grabbed her hand and held it tight in a moment of enlightenment.

Then they walked into an over-priced greasy spoon café overlooking the market square and ordered an all-day breakfast.

The Norma Red

Following the unsatisfying delight that passed itself as pig meat, toasted bread, some strange variety of bean, and an egg, Gertie suggested that they take a walk in a particularly desolated part of the market.

They took a left turn through some hanging carpets, past a spice stall, and then turned right into an, altogether, different experience. The light seemed to be darker in this part of the market, and the locals were not as frantic as they had seen earlier. The pace of life was slower here and the desire to sell their product not as great. This was not the Marrakesh meant for the tourists. No, this was the part of town that only the locals strayed upon.

And as they strolled slowly through the cramped alleyways the concentration of tourists lessened, and the concentration of distant un-welcoming natives increased.

'Look!' whispered Gertie in a semi-excited tone 'It's a picture of that car you like.' It was a picture of a Norma Red, and Gertie knew that the Norma Red was Mr P's favourite car of all time. He had seen it in an old human film and had been fascinated by it ever since.

'That is a superb thing. Can we go look?' he asked optimistically.

'Of course you can, only you're not buying one,' came the reply.

Slightly disappointed, but not surprised, he walked tentatively over to the shop window and peered inside. Not only was there a picture of a Norma Red, but there was a real life one. A real-life Norma Red right there in front of his googly eyes. This was too good to miss. He grabbed Gertie by the hand and walked inside.

'Heeelloooo,' came a voice from a rather shadowy character. 'My name is Kice, can I be of service?'

'That is a cool car, sir,' answered Mr P. 'Is it for sale?'

'But of course, sir, everything here is for sale but not everything that's for sale is here. I have more stuff in the back you see,' and with that Kice gestured his hand towards the Norma Red.

'That is so cool, Gertie. Have you seen anything so wonderful in your entire life?'

Now Gertie wasn't a car lover. In fact, there were very few things that got her excited. She was more of a practical Dinglewit who enjoyed the simple things in life.

'It is a very nice colour,' she answered, not wanting to seem rude.

'Nice colour! Babe it is immense.' He turned to Kice. 'Can I sit inside, sir?' he asked.

'Be my guest.'

A massive smile emerged on the face of Mr P and he, rather cautiously, got into the Norma Red and sat with both hands on the steering wheel facing forward. 'Is it a time machine?' He asked without moving his head.

'It is, sir,' came Kice's reply.

Now, time travel was banned, and had been banned for over a hundred years since it became obvious that Dinglewits were only travelling back in time to give themselves the lottery numbers. Therefore, time travel had been banned for the greater good, but not time machines, oh no, it is still legal to own a time machine , and in the eyes of Mr P, this is the coolest one that ever existed.

The reasoning behind not banning time machines was twofold. Firstly, you need more than a time machine to travel back in time; you also need a drink mixed from alcohol and Oobleck called Oocohol — and Oocohol IS banned. You see the problem with time travel is that you cannot pass through the continuum of time in a soft and squidgy state; only solids can pass through time. Therefore, Oocohol was invented to temporarily turn Dinglewits into a solid form while time travelling. There was no lasting deficit from this procedure and Oocohol only lasted for thirty minutes or so before everything returned to normal. How is this possible you might ask? Well, Dinglewits descended from frogs, and have the ability to freeze and un-freeze on occasions. It's in their genetic line-ology. Their genetic line-ology also accounts for their remarkable ability to taste revolting when licked.

Unfortunately, there are no known stocks of Oocohol on Earth since Greece tried to get hold of some to pay off their debts.

Apparently, there is a species in the Delta Pov system that does have some, but they don't understand its full potential and only use it at parties.

Oh and secondly, Cedar makes a lot of money from manufacturing time machines and wouldn't allow for a reduction in their industry.

'How much for the car?' asked Mr P. 'Five hundred Crowns,' came the reply.

Now in G-town 500 Crowns is the equivalent to one week's pay, but here in Marrakesh, it will feed a family of thirteen for a year.

He looked at Gertie. Gertie looked back.

'It is cheap babe. We may never get a better deal,' he pointed out.

'We!' stated Gertie, 'it's not we that want one, it's you.'

'But we have the money, babe,' Mr P responded, 'and didn't we always say that if you want something, and you can afford it, then you should buy it?'

There was truth in that. They had always gone on the premise that, if you can afford something and it will make you happy, then just go for it. And she supposed that this was one of those circumstances.

'Well, if you really want it, babe, then go for it.'

'I'll take it!' came the immediate response from Mr P.

Gertie sighed. Kice smiled. Mr P continued to smile for the rest of the holiday.

And with that he became Mr P — the ginger time traveller — and he was well happy. He paid the money, organised delivery, and then proudly walked out of the shop with a massive grin on his face.

Gertie was not so impressed, but she had agreed to the adventure, so she only had herself to blame, or so Mr P thought anyway.

But unbeknown to Mr P and Gertie there was more to Kice than first meets the eye. He wasn't just a car salesman in some dark and dank back street in a far-off land, but he was in fact, a professor. And Professor Kice was highly respected within the walls of the Great Library of Angar on the planet of Cedar. So why is he here? And why is he acting the part of a salesman?

Let's just say that his meeting with Mr P was not, exactly, accidental.

Time travel ain't what it used to be

It is a commonly believed myth that in order to travel back in time you need to travel at eighty-eight miles per hour. This is simply not true and you shouldn't believe everything you see in films.

Now time travel is not without its pitfalls. Many a clever Dinglewit have come unstuck navigating the space-time continuum — much to everyone's amusement. The problem lies in getting the speed exactly right as any miscalculation leads to a rather long and drawn-out death in the dark and lonely emptiness of the universe.

And nobody wants that!

The big problem is this — the Earth is located in an outer spiral arm of the Milky Way galaxy called the Orion spur located approximately 30,000 light years from the core. Within the Milky Way the Earth travels at 220 kilometres per second with the Milky Way itself travelling at 150 kilometres per second towards the Virgo cluster. This gives a combined speed of 370 kilometres per second for which any time traveller has to beat, in order to travel back in time, and get back again within a workable time frame.

The calculations need to be exact as well, and they are a bit tricky. For example, if you wish to travel back one hundred years, then firstly you need to work out the location of Earth one hundred years ago. That would be 31,536,000 kilometres per calendar year and 31,622,400 kilometres per leap year. It is normally calculating the leap years that allows for all the amusing deaths commonly seen on the televisions, as this varies depending on the number of years that you wish to travel for, and the year of which you are travelling to. You then project back along the curvature of the Earth's pattern through space, and plot the location of Earth in the universal location device.

Alternatively, you could go on the universal ethernet and look it up as it has already been calculated.

You then need a space ship that can travel faster than the required 370 kilometres per second or 827,666 miles per hour, and hey presto, you are a time traveller.

However, the difference in the speed in which you are travelling and the speed of the Earth needs to be calculated exactly or you will simply miss the Earth and die — eventually, and of course very slowly. This is another source of amusement for the Ethernet loving snuff aficionados, as it is quite tricky working out the acceleration velocity through the fluctuating universal time field. Oh, and I forgot to mention, you also need a fluctuating universal time field-suspending device.

The easier option of course is to buy a Norma Red, because it has a built-in flux-capacitor as standard.

Thus, time travel is possible — providing you can get Oocohol (which you can't). That being said, time is only a perception because everything that is happening is just a memory in those that were there at the time and therefore time travel is just a trip down memory lane really.

On Luyten b time travel is readily accessible because the Dinglewits have morphed themselves into a symbiotic relationship with computers, and are part of the universal web. This allows them to travel through the history that has been saved on the hard drive, without the perils normally attached with physical time travel. As yet though, the Dinglewits on Earth have resisted the temptation of forming a synergetic relationship with computers — much to the amusement of the elders back home.

The Circle of Time

Now there is nothing more relaxing than a Sunday spring morning walk. And it has become tradition for Mr P and Geoffrey to undertake such a weekly Sunday morning walk to the local shop to buy a newspaper; it is just better during springtime.

'I watched the ol' time travelling film "The Circlet Hoop" again last night' began Mr P as they turned left at his house and began walking down the road.

'Oh, I liked that one,' replied Geoffrey.

'Yeah, me too, but I picked up on some problems though, serious problems.'

'I know what you mean,' Geoffrey added. 'That bit where he gets his limbs cut off, that just cannot be right ya know. The part of the film in question is where Wilkes does not kill himself when he had been sent back in time to be killed. This began a series of events where young Wilkes was captured and had limbs cut off that then instantly materialised on old Wilkes. Honestly, that's what happened.'

'Yeah, the point of that is that when old Wilkes came back from the future it's not the same Wilkes that is in the past, there are now two different Wilkes's there,' Mr P said, 'so once old Wilkes came the future, there are now, in essence, two different people on two different paths in time. Like he had jumped onto a new space-time continuum platform?'

Geoffrey looked puzzled and asked, 'But does that depend on whether you buy into the parallel universe's argument or follow the self-consistency timelines argument?'

'Well... it may be neither,' Mr P answered, 'it may just be that time works on platforms and when you go back in time then you simply step on another platform but still in the same dimension.'

'But you are totally dismissing the grandfather paradox.'

'YES!' jumped in Mr P. 'The grandfather paradox is the biggest con that's ever been spun by film companies, just so that they can sell films with storylines.'

'Absolutely,' agreed Geoffrey. 'It just looks better on films that a time traveller disappears when the past is interfered with, but in reality, that would never happen.'

Mr P agreed.

'Take the Circlet Hoop for example,' he said. 'If they were to write on young Wilkes's arm for old Wilkes to read, then they would need to capture young Wilkes, write on his arm, and then release him to let him live his life until he became THE old Wilkes, and then it may be possible, perhaps.'

'No that doesn't work,' interrupted Geoffrey. 'Because both Wilkes's would now know that he had been caught and would change their behaviour so as not to get caught in the first place.'

'True, and that's ignoring the fact that they then started cutting his fingers off, and then limbs off, which everyone will see and know why. Which is bound to change his future actions,' added Mr P. 'You can't just simply bypass the thirty years that happened since you started cutting off limbs, as if people's actions would not have changed as a result of YOUR actions.'

'Actions have consequences,' said Geoffrey.

'Correct, and so by cutting off young Wilkes's limbs you are basically changing the future. And that is, if you believe in the Hawking's chronology conjecture, which I don't, is why the film falls flat on its face,' answered Mr P.

'And that's forgetting the biggest error of the film,' added Geoffrey, 'and that is, that later on in the film young Booth killed old Booth by shooting himself, and he simply just disappeared from time. So by their own thought process, if they wanted to get rid of old Wilkes then they should have just shot young Wilkes and the whole thing would be over, simple.'

'Yeah, the film was inconsistent, but, also wrong because once you travel back in time you are further along the arrow of time and therefore not influenced by what has already happened. Not immediately anyway,' added Mr P.

'It's all about your perception of time, dude,' intervened Geoffrey, 'if you perceive time as one continuous loop that can be influenced anywhere along that loop, and which has an immediate effect from the exact point where the interaction happened, then it IS possible to immediately change the future person.'

'But that's not taking into account the timeline that the original person already had. They can't be simply deleted because they actually happened and they interfered with other timelines. It simply can't happen, it can't just be deleted,' said Mr P.

Now Geoffrey, being the great storyteller he was, chose to take the side of the film writers on this.

'Well, writing stories can take science at its word only so far you see. And after that, a tad of artistic toting is required,' he added.

'Well, my good friend, I shall leave that in your capable mind. Let us grab a coffee and a newspaper,' Mr P concluded.

The shop was empty on that Sunday morning and Geoffrey decided to get a Turkish Delight for the walk home. Mr P got a Bounty.

But the conversation got Mr P thinking about his mission on finding the meaning to life, and this appeared to be as good a place as any to start.

The rest of the walk was in quiet reflection, but once home Mr P got a notebook and a green crayon and wrote:

The meaning of life — 1) Be inquisitive

It's important to have perspective in life, but Cyclops struggle

Upon their first visit to Earth, some 16,000 years ago, Dinglewits attempted to teach the Earthlings how to build a civilised societal system based on merit, hard work, or how much wealth you are born with.

The Dinglewits helped with pyramid building, and showed them how to make creatures out of the rocks, that look really cool, and will last for thousands of years. However, the inhabitants of Tiahuanaco chose to worship them as gods, and so the Dinglewits left to seek a more intellectually comparable life form.

What they found was a Cyclops abomination that kept walking into things. It's important to have perspective, but for that you need both eyes open.

Dinglewits know this, being as they are, the most intellectually superior species in the cosmos. 'We must be,' they think, 'because we are capable of travelling between the stars.' A thing they have been doing for years now, although there have been a few slip-ups along the way. The arse job they made in turning Venus into a surfer's paradise, whereby they were forced to transport water from Mars but ended up in making both planets inhospitable. But Dinglewits are a pragmatic species that wouldn't let something as trivial as planetary doom dissuade them from something enjoyable.

A Dinglewit once wrote 'you are born with nothing, so if you die owing money, you have made a profit.' So to that particular Dinglewit, perspective gave him a licence to be a miserable git. It takes all sorts.

But it was a shame that the Tiahuanaco people preferred to treat the Dinglewits as gods, because on board the mother ship were the Flying Willybums from the planet Gliese 445 Alpha 6, that were being given a lift on their way to the Orion nebula — and were looking forward to visiting Sardinia — they had heard it was good this time of the year. An even bigger shame is that the Flying Willybums had erotic strippers on board that are generally regarded as the most sensual of all bipedal species. The humans would have been in awe of their beauty, but as it was, the humans of Tiahuanaco were too busy on their knees praying, and so missed probably the greatest striptease act in the entire galaxy.

A delivery

Mr P and Gertie had been home for a couple of days when a letter was delivered in the morning post. The envelope had tape all around the edges and looked like it had been to the sun and back — twice. Mr P fondled the package and noted that there was something hard in the middle of it.

'Gertie,' he shouted, 'come and see this.'

Gertie walked into the hallway and took hold of the envelope, while pulling up the back of her pyjama bottoms because they get stuck around her feet. 'Oooh, who's this from?' Gertie asked.

'It's just come in the post. I'm not expecting anything, have you ordered something from Titan again?'

Gertie was always ordering stuff from Titan because of the cheap price. Titan is basically a massive sweatshop where the daily wage is so low that no other company in the universe can compete. Companies on Titan sell everything from cheap tat to expensive spaceships, all at a fraction of the price of companies elsewhere. That being said, the quality is somewhat questionable, and ethically there are issues, but hey, it's cheap. The result, however, has resulted in Titan being the powerhouse of the Milky Way for which all other planets depend, and as such, behave in a way akin to a dictatorship. I'm sure there will be problems before too long; especially when the galactic superpower that is Luyten b decides enough is enough. But anyway, back to the mysterious package.

'No,' said Gertie, 'I haven't ordered anything recently, not since that novelty bottle opener that doubles up as a gun. Open it!'

Mr P sat on the bottom of the stairs and took a pair of scissors from the sideboard, cut one end of the package, and tipped the contents onto the floor. The envelope contained a coin, a map, and a note. Mr P picked up the note first. It read:

Dear Mr P

It is with many thanks for your purchase of the Norma Red time machine and I hope it is everything you wished for. As you may be aware, you cannot time travel without Oocohol but as it happens, I have a friend that may be willing to trade some.

I have attached a map of his whereabouts, although he is very cautious about the company he keeps. If you say that you know me, he should be more inviting. I have sent you a coin that may help.

Happy travels.

With very gracious thoughts.

Kice

'Wow' said Mr P. 'It's a treasure map!!'

'Well, not exactly a treasure map,' replied Gertie, 'but exciting nevertheless, what you gonna do?'

'I think we should go, it could be fun. And it could be helpful to find the meaning of life, or, maybe going on adventures is the meaning of life, babe,' came the excited reply.

'OK, OK, calm yourself,' replied Gertie, 'pass me the map.'

The map was hand written on a parchment of hemp paper. It looked old, and had been stored for some time. Also, X marked the spot.

Mr P liked maps where X marks the spot. 'Where is it asking you to go to?' asked Gertie.

'There's no start point,' replied Mr P. 'We need to figure out where to start, but if we do that, it all looks pretty straightforward.'

'What's on the coin, maybe there is a clue there,' Gertie suggested.

'Mmm, looks like a picture of cliff,' replied Mr P.

Gertie took the coin for a closer inspection. 'I'll tell you exactly where that is,' she exclaimed rather excitedly. 'That is Pedn Vounder.'

'How on Earth do you know that?' came the shocked response.

'Because I've been there,' she continued, 'when we were kids, Dad took us on a tour of some of the cliffs around the dragon sanctuary, and that was one that has stuck in my head. I think the reason why I remember it is because of a strange cave on the ocean side of Logan rock that sticks out about 100 metres from the mainland. It seemed that someone had lived there at some point in time, which always fascinated me. I always felt that the dragons were guarding them or something silly.'

'Well, if that's the starting point then X is on that very cave,' Mr P explained.

The two looked at each other as if fate had meant for them to do this. There was no way they weren't going. This was an opportunity to travel in time, and if this mysterious friend of Kice's was willing to give them some Oocohol, then it could actually happen.

A sense of excitement gripped the air.

'We leave in the morning, Gertie,' said Mr P.

'Or right now!' Gertie added, now getting more enthused than Mr P had ever seen her before, 'why bother waiting for the morning? Let's go!' And with that she walked upstairs to pack some clothes.

Mr P sat back on the stairs, got out his notebook, and wrote:

The meaning of life — 2) Be adventurous

'Yes,' he said, 'adventure is so instinctive that it must be a part of the meaning of life.'

And with that Mr P and Gertie packed their bags in anticipation of an adventure.

Logey

Logey the campervan was packed to the rafters with enough food for ten Dinglewits for ten years, and yet they were only travelling 300 miles down the coast.

They were going on an adventure that involved a map marked with an X that led to a secret cave, where they could buy a rare liquid, so they could go time travelling.

This was living. And as they set off it was a warm sunny evening and they would reach their destination at Pedn Vounder by dusk.

They decided to take two vehicles, Mr P was going to drive the Norma Red and Gertie was taking Logey the campervan.

Logey had been around the block a few times and he was temperamental too. Sometimes the side door would work and sometimes it wouldn't. Sometimes the heater worked and sometimes it didn't. But since Logey was part of the family it simply couldn't be changed or upgraded. Besides, Logey the campervan was a rare limited edition Artificial Intelligent van that was made and bought by Mr P before they were banned following the Great A.I. War. The only reason why Logey is still allowed to exist is because he was an early model that is not capable of universal thought intelligence, but is merely task programmed. Even so, he was a very clever old bean that knew his way to every mapped destination, and some that aren't.

Pedn Vounder at sunrise is a sight to behold, and Mr P and Gertie were sat looking at Logan Rock eating bacon sandwiches and pondering the events of the day. The map was pretty straightforward when you had the starting place. It was a walk along the top of Logan Rock and down the ocean side to an abandoned cave, then enter through the cave entrance on the side of the ocean, and continue downward to an underground lagoon. Simple. Simple, apart from one thing — dragons — and lots of them.

Now dragons have a very bad reputation due to the fact that they breathe fire and are very territorial. If attacked they will certainly breath fire on you and have a barbecued Dinglewit for lunch. They may even invite a few friends round and make a day of it. But if left alone, and not spooked in any way, then they tend to just go about their business of eating fish and sleeping.

They can fly long distances, but choose not to as they prefer to eat the local fish around the edges of the cliff. And as for the fire breathing, well, they prefer not to do that either as it uses up a lot of energy, and then they have to sleep for several hours afterwards.

The dragons around Pedn Vounder are unique in the sense as not all dragons can breathe fire. The reason these dragons can is due to the unique make-up of

Logan Rock that the dragons choose to chew on. This led to a whole host of conspiracy theories as Logan Rock is not local to these cliffs, or anywhere else to be exact. In fact, there is no other rock with the same formation as Logan Rock anywhere else on earth. This led to theories that it was transported from another planet, or maybe it was a meteorite, or maybe it was moved there from another dimension. Either way it's the rock that allows the dragons to breathe fire, and Pedn Vounder is a sanctuary for dragons.

This is a problem for Mr P and Gertie.

'How are we going to get past them?' asked Gertie, 'they look scary.'

'I'm not sure,' replied Mr P. 'Perhaps if we move very slowly at night time then they might not see us.'

'Well, what if they do? They will kill us.'

'Yeah, probably.'

They both stared at the scene of dragons in front of them on the beach. In the middle was the queen dragon. She was gloriously white with bright red tipped feathers, and she controlled the pack. The rumour is, that if a pack of dragons go on a feeding frenzy, then only the queen can stop them. All the dragons live to serve their queen, and only their queen.

Dragons

The sandy beach at Pedn Vounder stretches for 200 metres from side to side surrounded by high rocks. Logan Rock was to the left of the beach, it is possible that by clambering silently along the top of the rocks the dragons won't see them, and then they could enter the cave through the entrance on the other side. This was probably their only plan, and was it literally a matter of life and death.

Mr P needed inspiration. He looked into his notebook and saw that he had written "Be adventurous" as the second meaning of life. He smirked to himself "be adventurous, sure, but not suicidal", and this seemed suicidal.

He showed his notebook to Gertie. 'Be adventurous?' she said in a questionable tone. 'Yep, this is definitely what you could call adventurous, that's for sure.'

'And bloody dangerous as well, Gertie. Shall we do this?'

'Well, we have come all this way,' she replied.

'But not to be eaten by fire-breathing dragons though.'

He sat down, got out his clay pipe, and proceeded to have a smoke. Probably his last ever smoke. So he overfilled it with his very favourite blend of shag. Struck a match, and took in a deep breath.

Gertie sat next to him; she loved the smell of his pipe.

Although the sun was beginning to rise it was still dark and the darkness gave them the cover that they needed. It wouldn't be long before the sun shone fully onto the glorious Cornish coastline and then they would be like sitting ducks.

The decision had been made. They were going to go for it. Mr P had conceived that they were nice Dinglewits, and nice things always happened to nice Dinglewits. Sort of like fate, but not really.

And so, with backpacks packed in case they get stranded and a torch on the dimmest setting they began the walk across the top of the rocks. Not forgetting the coin of course, the letter had stated that the coin could come in useful.

'Do you think his friend is still there, babe?' asked Gertie as they struggled over the unstable rocks overlooking the beach.

'Well, Kice said he was, and he seemed pretty legit,' replied Mr P.

'I'm nervous,' came the response.

'Me too, Gertie, me too.' Mr P admitted, 'but what an adventure eh?'

As they slowly walked over the rocks, they could see the dragons below them stirring. The queen was being protected by several of her army dragons but she seemed relaxed. Mr P and Gertie kept low and slowly, but surely, made their way along the top of the cliffs. Surprisingly their plan seemed to be working and as they approached the edge leading to the edge of Logan Rock not a single dragon was interested in their actions.

Mr P looked down and could see a very thin path that led to the entrance of the cave. 'There it is, Gertie, we need to get to that entrance,' explained Mr P.

'That looks dangerous,' Gertie whispered just loud enough for Mr P to hear.

'Do you want to stay up here? It's OK if you do,' Mr P asked.

'No, I'm coming with you,' Gertie said determined to be a part of this adventure.

She often missed out on events because she did not enjoy being out of her comfort zone, but this time she was in, and was going to see it through.

They slowly, but surely, clambered their way down the ocean side of the rock being very careful not to lose their footing. Neither were, what you would call, outdoorsy Dinglewits, and so this was quite a task for them. Nevertheless within an hour they had conquered the rock face and were now in the cave entrance. The dragons hadn't stirred.

Mr P got the map from his bag. 'The arrows point in here and down into this cave,' Mr P explained.

'Jeez, it looks dark, babe,' Gertie answered, 'let's hope we have enough batteries.

'God yeah, I never thought of that,' answered Mr P. 'Ready?

'Let's go,' came the response.

Mr P was quite surprised by the braveness of Gertie, as she was normally quite timid.

And so, with a touch of hands, they tentatively began into the darkness of the cave.

Strange little creature

The cave was dark and the rocks that made up the roof were jagged and sharp. The atmosphere inside was humid and with water droplets dripping down the sides of the cave. They made a plopping sound as they hit the small puddles that they had created. As they walked further down the cave the light from the entrance became fainter and fainter. Gertie grabbed hold of Mr P's coat.

After about 100 metres there was a sharp turn to the right and into total blackness. 'Ooh, babe, I don't like this,' said Gertie now quite scared.

They stopped and took another look at the map.

'It's just down here according to the map,' said Mr P, 'let's continue a bit further and see how you feel, eh.'

'I ain't turning back now,' she stated in a determined voice, 'after you!'

And she pushed Mr P in the back to move him forward and into the dark. With a few more tentative steps they found the spiral rocky steps that lead down to the secret lagoon. And it was only a short time later, and a few more tentative steps, that there was light, and the light was beautiful.

It was a reflective and kind light, the sort that you get as the afternoon sun reflects off a perfectly clear lake, and where the ripples of the water cause a moving of the wavelengths. The flowing light was a welcome sight and they could see the sides to the cave, as they shone. The stoned walls were smooth, as if thousands of years of hands brushing over them had taken away the rough edges. And every metre, or so, there was a hand drawn diagram like someone decorating the walls to a hallway. They followed the steps down, and as they did, they could see the lagoon with multi-coloured lights bouncing from its surface. The water rocked ever so slightly from some unforeseen influence, and was totally clear.

Beside the lagoon was a small hut made from bamboo and other types of wood, and sat inside was the shape of a very small creature.

'Hello!' called out Mr P. 'We come in peace. We are friends of Kice.'

'Whaaaat,' shouted the figure as they suddenly jumped up from their lounger, 'what are you doing here? Go away,' the mysterious figure continued.

'My name is Mr P, and this is Gertie. We are friends of Kice, and he said that you can help us,' Mr P answered.

'Kice... never heard of him,' came the immediate response. 'What do you want?' Mr P put both hands outstretched in a friendly and welcoming manner.

'Kice said that you have Oocohol,' replied Mr P, 'that's all, we mean you no harm. I have a time machine you see, but I need some Oocohol, Kice said that you have some that you may be willing to trade.'

The mysterious creature moved closer to Mr P and Gertie, and looked them up and down. 'And what do you have to trade?' came the irritated response.

'Well, I have money, how much does it cost?' Mr P suggested, rather nervously.

The idea of money did not help in the slightest. It was apparent from his way of life that money was of no use to him. He lived in the middle of nowhere, he was obviously a hermit, and besides, he could not get to spend it in a shop even if there was one nearby due to his appearance.

'What do I want money for?' said the creature. 'I have no use for money. Go away.' And he pulled his hood over his head and turned away.

Hanging all around the cave were various types of sleep catchers that all looked hand made. They all looked old as well thought Mr P. This creature obviously has a spiritual side to him, he thought. He moved towards a giant sleep catcher of multi-colours that seemed to be Arabic in style. There may even have been some Egyptian influence in there somewhere. He reached out and brushed his fingers over the fine threads that made up the web. But as he brushed, the webs seemed to dissipate and float around, before re-assembling once the chubby fingers had passed.

'Oh wow!' he said in amazement, 'what are these?'

The creature stopped and looked around. He removed his hood, and his manner calmed. He moved closer to Mr P. 'Those are dream catchers,' he said, 'but not the type that you buy in solstice shops. Oh no, they are the original thing. Made from dreams.'

Mr P's eyes fixed wide open. His pupils dilated. And his mouth opened, ever so slightly.

'That is so cool,' he said, 'they look old.'

'They are old,' answered the creature, 'because dreams are old. Since time eternal, every living life form has had dreams. And here are some of mine. Captured for prosperity.'

'So these are your dreams?' asked Mr P. 'Wow, how do you make them?'

'Not all of these are my dreams,' he answered, 'some of these dreams are from loved ones. Loved ones that are no longer here you see. And while I have these, I have, at least, some connection with them.'

Mr P thought this was a bit kooky, if he was being honest, but still, the thought of being able to capture dreams and emotions was a really neat idea. 'And do you make these yourself?' Mr P asked.

'Yes. It's easy if you have the soul to do it.'

Sensing that this was a good time to move the conversation forward, Gertie stepped forward and pulled the coin out of the pocket of Mr P. 'We have this coin,' she stated. 'We think it has a meaning, will this suffice as payment for the Oocohol?' she continued.

The creature stepped forward and put out its hand. A smile appeared on its face, and the atmosphere became immediately friendly. 'You have a coin! Oh, my goodness, yes. How did you get hold of a coin?'

'Kice gave us it,' answered Gertie. 'He said that you might be willing to trade it for Oocohol.'

'Kice gave you a coin?' the creature asked. 'Now why on Earth would Kice give you a coin?'

'I don't know,' replied Mr P, 'he just sent it in the post along with a map of this cave. Do you know Kice then?'

'I do,' answered the creature, 'we go back a long way. A long, long way... Oh and by the way,' he continued, 'my name is Percival! Please, wait here.'

Percival then turned and walked into a small hiding that had strips of red ribbons hanging from the top that served as, a sort of, partition, all the while not taking his eyes off the coin.

Gertie turned to Mr P. 'Oh, my goodness,' she muttered, 'this place is awesome. We could live here forever, babe.'

Mr P was not quite so keen. But before he could put his foot in his mouth, Percival returned holding a bottle of liquid. 'Please take,' he said, passing the bottle to Mr P, 'and please, if it isn't too much to ask, would you mind leaving now? I haven't had many visitors down here over the years you see. And I'm not really used to entertaining guests.'

Gertie smiled, and gave Percival her best friendly look. The look she normally reserves for her grandmother. 'Well, you did great, Percival,' she assured him, and not wishing to outstay their welcome, they slowly turned and walked back towards the way that they had come in.

On the way out, Mr P couldn't resist pushing his fingers through the dream catchers, and then watching them reform.

Gertie slapped his arm. 'Stop it!' she insisted. Mr P did as he was told.

They didn't speak as they slowly strolled to the exit of the cave, but just as they approached the steps, Gertie stopped, and looked back. 'Are you going to be OK?' she asked.

Percival didn't reply; he just sat back into his seat, not taking his eyes off the coin and looking very pleased with his new acquisition.

And with that, they left, and assuredly walked back to the entrance of the cave.

Before long they were scrambling their way up the face of Logan Rock and back to where Logey the campervan had been waiting patiently for their return.

They were tired and full of adrenaline, but, as they sat on the back step of Logey, breathing hard and sweating, Gertie turned to Mr P and asked, 'What was that strange little creature?'

There was a silence for a few seconds. 'I think it was a human!'

Zombie ants

To achieve meaning, it is necessary to first achieve thinking, and not just any old thinking, but original thinking. The problem is original thought is difficult, and not well tolerated by the authoritarian establishments. For an example of this just look at Copernicus and Galileo from human history, they had surmised that mainstream ideas were wrong, but were still ridiculed for their judgements, and even run out of town on pains of death.

Now it is true that ridicule is nothing to be scared of, but nevertheless, when the whole of society is against you, because you question their belief patterns, then original thought is nearly always victimised. When you study the history of all of the developed civilisations to have ever existed it begs the question of whether we are truly free to engage in original thought, or, are even the most pioneering of thinkers still caged within the parameters of their societal conscience.

Now the universal brain is very consistent, being that it is made up from different areas of matter with differing voltage thresholds that communicate with each other through neurons that release chemicals. Decision-making is primarily made within the areas of the Anterior Cingulate Cortex and the Ventromedial Prefrontal Cortex that themselves receive signals from the Dorsolateral Prefrontal and the Orbitofrontal Cortices. And neurons that fire together wire together, which allows for the structure of brain processing. This is consistent within the universal brain. And if any part of the brain is under-developed then the activity that that particular area evokes is reduced — or even absent.

In Dinglewits the Dorsolateral Prefrontal Cortex is not as large as in other species and no one knows, or has even thought to ask, why. The Dorsolateral Prefrontal Cortex is found to regulate cravings, and is important in the ability to stop or modify planned behaviour. Where and when this deficit in the Dinglewit brain matter occurred is unknown, but because there is scarcity of the Prefrontal Cortex no one is actually asking the question.

The evolution, or manipulation, of the Dorsolateral Prefrontal Cortex is vital in the free thought of species and its capacity to ask questions of its purpose, a fact not forgotten by those at the top of the food chain.

Mr P had recently read about a fungus called Ophiocordyceps unilateralis (or just plain Cordyceps to those in the business) that infects ants and hijacks their brains. These ants are sometimes called "zombie ants" because the fungus completely changes their personalities and characteristics and makes them behave in a peculiar way. The Cordyceps fungus does eventually kill the ants by draining their body of nutrients, but hey-ho, it's a means to an end.

Now if a fungus can infect an ant and change its behaviour then has this ever happened to a species further up the food chain? Is it possible that we are merely the result of fungal architecture, or even the product of viral construction patterns?

The problem is when you are personally invested in a certain train of thought it is almost impossible to deviate from it and see things that appear alien. This "original thought catastrophe" correlates with advanced society, and therefore, to truly achieve original thought one may have to leave society.

Sat on the tip of Logan Rock at Pedn Vounder Mr P and Gertie were temporarily absent from society.

And absent from society they would remain. At least for the time being anyway. And this got Mr P thinking about the meaning of life again. If they were going to time travel and meet Dinglewits from the past, whom should they meet?

Everybody is well aware of ancient philosophers and leaders who engraved their beliefs on society, but what about Dinglewits from more obscure backgrounds.

'If I am to truly discover the meaning of life, babe, perhaps I should talk to ordinary Dinglewits. You know, the ones that had lived experiences, normal experiences. Like musicians or nurses,' said Mr P. 'What about the singer Madame Denier, babe?'

'Denier!' replied Gertrude. 'D'ya mean that very loud and eccentric singer from the olden days?'

'Yeah! Ya know, "don't you step on my eight toed feet" and all that,' Mr P replied. 'She was a genius, loved by everyone on the planet. She must have had some experiences and can tell us about the meaning of life.'

Now to some Dinglewits meeting Madame Denier may not be the most obvious choice when trying to find the meaning of life, but to Mr P it made perfect sense. The young ones loved her, all pensioners loved her, so therefore she must have had something magical, and having something magical is a part of existence.

'Every single creature in the universe has something magic about him or her, Gertie. Every single creature is unique in their own way. Every single creature is capable of great things. They may never understand this fact, or ever be aware of it, but they do. Perhaps the meaning of life is understanding this fact.'

Mr P was getting philosophical now, and this scared Gertie — but in a nice way.

Mr P continued. 'Everybody wants to be considered magical, everybody wants to be adored, and everybody wants to achieve something great. Madame Denier did all those things, and in spades.'

He reached over to pick up a bottle of home brew, and continued. 'When you see the young kiddiedingles that are not influenced by life, and the drudgery of existence, what do you see?' he asked.

'Innocence!' replied Gertie.

'Exactly, they behave like unicorns, or an ancient knight in shining armour, or magical and mythical creatures that can fly and do amazing things,' Mr P persisted. 'Maybe that's what life is all about! I'm gonna write that down.'

He reached in his pocket for his notebook, and with his green crayon wrote:

The meaning of life — 3) Be magical

'Yes, being magical is definitely something we should be,' Gertie replied.

The lagoon of eternal life

It was a warm night and with winds blowing from the west. 'Why are you writing in green crayon?' Gertie asked.

'Because everything that is important should be written in green crayon, babe,' came his rather enthusiastic reply.

Gertie agreed. The universe is too full of black pens and alphabetical storage devices. What are needed are more unicorns, pink fluffy dragons, and transcripts written in green crayon. That is the universe that Gertie wanted to live in, and in that universe, she would share it with Mr P.

'So what do you reckon, babe?' asked Mr P. 'SWhall we go and see Madame Denier?'

Gertie sat in silence for a moment to think about it. For sure Madame Denier would not have been her first choice, or indeed, in her top one hundred, but meeting a superstar is appealing. But, as she sat there thinking of another option, it became clear that all the influential figures of universal history were human, none were Dinglewits.

Gertie could not think of a single Dinglewit that had changed their world — whichever world they were living on — as much as a human had. The Dinglewit race merely accepted the narrative and got on with life. Any change was slow, selected through committee, and instigated by proportional representation. There had never been an uprising, or a bottom-up revolution of the poor. Life and death may as well be charted on a graph for nearly all Dinglewits to follow, and everyone accepted their fate. Apart from the rich and powerful that is.

Mr P and Gertie, and all their family members, were on that very same trajectory where they were expected to accept the mainstream narrative and not rock the boat.

Gertie looked inquisitively at Mr P. 'If it's a musician that you're thinking about meeting, what about Simonides of Ceos or Orpheus? Or if you want to talk art then go for Apelles or Zeuxis, or if you're interested in talking politics then go for Hammurabi or Sutch?' she said. 'All these great men lived interesting lives. They will all have a different view on what is the meaning of life. Just picking one who basically lived in a rock 'n' roll bubble would not offer a variation that you may be looking for.'

Mr P looked out into the ocean without saying a word. He so badly wanted to meet Madame Denier, and isn't this what life is all about, doing the things you want to do regardless of how sensible or non-productive it is, but he also knew that it would probably be a waste to use the Oocohol on meeting the woman who sang "dog paws" and "tender toes", and that perhaps he should use this gift wisely.

Right at that exact moment a comet lit up the sky. It seemed like a sign. A gift from the gods to two ordinary bipedal life forms that had started to question their reality and look for meaning.

'That's comet Hale-Bopp, Gertie,' said Mr P. 'It's on its 2500 and something year orbit of the Earth, I heard it was due about now, this is a sign.'

'Now, now, don't be getting excited,' chipped in Gertie.

She knew this was an important moment and she didn't need Mr P rushing into something silly, a thing he was prone to do.

She continued, 'That comet is on an orbital path and it's just coincidence that we are sat here when it appeared.'

She knew that was not going to wash but felt it was worth a try.

'Here, have another drink,' she said.

'No it's a gift, babe,' said Mr P.

And with that he stood up and looked out onto the large expanse of water and turned to Gertie. 'I know what we must do, grab your things.'

Gertie did not question the decision. She knew he had made an executive decision, and although this didn't happen very often, when he did, he would not be deterred. They headed back to the cave at Logan Rock, it seemed easier the second time around, and as they walked into the darkness again the feelings of fear had gone.

'I feel at ease,' said Gertie.

'That's because once something has been experienced the fear of the unknown doesn't exist,' replied Mr P.

'No,' came the reply, 'this is different, I feel we are about to do something special.'

Mr P looked at Gertie and with a wry friendly smile said, 'Me too, babe, me too.'

They retraced their steps into the cave, around the corner into the darkness, and down the steps to the lagoon. As the light that reflected from the water lit up the cave, they could see Percival sat on a rock looking intensely at the coin.

'I'm sorry to bother you again, Percival,' called Mr P, 'but I feel there is something we missed.'

Percival looked up and put the coin in his pocket. They weren't changing the deal on the coin. That was for sure. But he didn't look afraid or troubled by the re-appearance of the couple, as if he knew that they were good people and would not do any harm.

'How can I help you?' asked Percival.

'You can't,' said Mr P. 'It is us that can help you.'

'How so?' came the inquisitive response and with a grin on his face. Mr P approached Percival and gave him a key.

'You don't belong here, Percival, and if my instincts are right, you did something to help another and this is the result. How long have you been here?'

Percival nodded his head.

'Too long, my strange friend, way too long.' Mr P knew it. 'And I guess you couldn't leave because you didn't have a time machine, and clearly, you are not from this time,' he stated clearly, but in a questionable tone.

'Sometimes life throws a curve ball, I wouldn't change it, but I do miss them dearly.' Shrugged Percival. 'What is the key for?' he asked.

Mr P took a few steps back and with a deep breath said, 'At the top of Logan Rock there is a Norma Red car. It is a time machine and that is the key, on the front seat is the Oocohol you gave us. It's yours. Go back to them.'

Percival was speechless and just stood motionless at the edge of the lagoon. Mr P and Gertie silently turned and walked away leaving Percival to hope on his future.

As they began walking back up the steps Percival spoke. 'Did you know that the water in here keeps you young and alive forever?'

'Err no,' replied Gertie in a friendly manner, talking as if the two of them were old friends.

Percival walked forward. 'It's because of the rock you see. It's from an alien species that paid a passing visit to Earth. No one has yet discovered this place. Can you imagine if news ever got out? The aliens visited here thousands of years ago and used this lagoon as a, sort of, restoration site where the water repaired the damage that the atmosphere caused to their bodies.'

Mr P and Gertie were clearly amazed by this. They walked over to the pool of water and looked in. It was clear and you could see all the way down to the bottom of the seabed. There was a shining reflection to the water that you don't normally see and there appeared to be slightly different streams of colours moving through that is not too obvious to the casual observer.

Percival continued, 'The rock is special. As the water seeps through its pores, it is galvanised with nutrients and goodness not of this planet, or any other in the known universe. If you swim in it every day you will lengthen your life, and you certainly feel better and healthier. I have swum in it every single day since I discovered it. Under normal circumstances this would have been a good thing but for me it has only prolonged my loneliness and suffering. But it seems that it bought me time for you two to find me and give me a chance to see my family again.'

Mr P smiled. He doesn't normally get emotional, he isn't the emotional type, but even he knew that this was a poignant moment. 'How many people know of this place?' he asked.

Percival turned and sat down on a rock that had been shaped into a chair over thousands of years of being sat upon. 'Well,' he said 'no one has been here for the years that I have been here, so I would guess that no one else knows.'

'No one except us three then!' answered Mr P.

They all looked at each other for one final time before Mr P and Gertie walked back up the steps and out of the cave.

Number 4 — Be nice

They drove Logey the campervan about a mile to the other side of the rock and rested up for the night. They weren't worried about being eaten in the night by flying dragons any more. They concluded that dragons were really friendly, well, those dragons were, and that myths and legends can be wrong sometimes. And in the case of the fire-breathing dragons of Pedn Vounder, the myths were definitely wrong.

They didn't speak much, and as the sun set over the most beautiful place on Earth, Mr P and Gertie went to sleep in each other's arms looking out at the ocean.

The following morning, they awoke to the sound of water crashing onto rocks. It was a wonderful morning and they both felt a sense of calm and happiness. They quietly packed up their blankets and pillows and headed back to the other side of the rock where they had left the Norma Red for Percival.

But it was gone, and in its place was a rather large rock with a sword leant up against it that sparkled in the morning sun. It was a bit of a mystery how Percival had carried a rock of that size and placed it where he had, but I suppose if you are motivated to do something, then anything is possible.

But as for the sword, well that was awesome thought Mr P. They parked up a few metres away, and walked over to take a look.

Leant up against the large rock was a beautiful shining silver sword. It had inscriptions down the length of one side in an ancient foreign tongue. The words seemed to have too many letters in, and most of them were symbols of some sort. 'This looks like Gaelic writing or something, Gertie, look,' Mr P stated, beckoning Gertie to have a closer look at the writing.

'Hmm, I don't think so babe. It looks like writing from another world,' she answered, 'the letters, they don't seem to match anything I have seen before. They are more like symbols than letters.'

She took hold of the sword and moved it around to get a better look at the inscriptions. 'Well,' she muttered, 'I don't think this type of metal is of this planet either. Verrrrry strange.'

She put down the sword and saw that Percival must have given them the coin back too. 'Babe, look, the coin.' She picked it up. 'I think it's the same one that we gave Percival. He's given it back to us.'

'Oh, he obviously doesn't want it then,' Mr P responded. 'The cheeky git though, he could have just taken it with him and got rid of it later.'

'No, babe, I think it's important, and that's why he has given us it back. I think he is thanking us with the coin.'

'Oh yeah, I didn't think of that,' Mr P answered, he could be a bit slow on the uptake at times.

Underneath the coin was a note. Gertie bent down and picked it up.

My good friends,

This coin is yours I believe.

It has more value than you could ever know, and it belongs with you. It is very rare, and it has abilities yet to be discovered.

Be careful of its power. Good luck with your travels Percival

'Well, there you go,' said Mr P. 'A magic coin and an alien sword. Not a bad day's work, is it?'

'Not forgetting the meeting with a human, eh,' replied Gertie.

'Oh yeah.'

'And not forgetting the lagoon of eternal life as well.'

'Oh God, yeah,' said Mr P. 'We must remember that for when we get old.'

Gertie smiled forlornly, 'Getting old, eh,' she answered, 'you don't like that idea very much do you?'

'No,' answered Mr P, 'I do not. I don't much like the idea of death. It needs to end I think.'

Gertie laughed. 'You are silly,' she commented.

Mr P walked over to Logey and pulled out a long leather strap. He tied it around the sword, and then strapped the sword to his back. 'Ehhh!' he said with a big grin on his face, 'how about this then. Don't I look cool?'

He made gestures like he had seen in old Kung Fu movies, and started strutting around like a super hero.

'I could be... Mr P... the warrior king,' he proclaimed, and started making martial art moves.

Gertie laughed at his prancing about. And she decided to sit on the grass and watch. She knew that this could take a while.

'I love this sword, babe. I'm going to call it... Excalibur... yes that's it. Excalibur, that's the name of my sword.'

Gertie shook her head in bemusement. She never quite understood why he had to give everything a name. She often thought that it's because he doesn't have many friends that he has to name everything. But in a cute sort of way, she quite enjoyed the names he came up with. So she let it go.

Mr P continued with his self-flattery. 'I am King P!' he shouted. 'King of the peoples of G-Town!'

He then attempted to pull out his sword from the makeshift sword sheath, but failed as it had been bound too tight, and he fell to the floor in a heap.

Gertie laughed again.

'Babe, help?' he yelled, as his head was burrowing its way into the soil.

'Nope,' she replied, 'this is much more fun.'

He struggled for a few seconds before emerging with a mouth full of grass. He spat them out and set about correcting his sheath.

'We did good today, babe, didn't we?' Gertie asked.

'We certainly did. It felt good to help Percival.'

'Yes, it did.'

They continued to chat for a while as Mr P mended his pride, until, as the evening light broke, they headed back to Logey the campervan to make their way home. But not before Mr P pulled out his notebook once again, and with his green crayon wrote:

The meaning of life — 4) Be Nice

Amatory siphonophores

The Dinglewit species had visited planet Earth way before the mass exodus occurred. The aim, then, was to educate the primitive humans, and allow them to grow into an independent space-faring life form, and contributing to the greater good of the universe. Unfortunately, this didn't turn out as planned. In fact, that initial Dinglewit expedition was considered such a disaster that its captain, Captain Edward Von Smoan, was immediately fired from his post, and replaced with a Flying Willybum captain, whose name cannot be written with letters. It is best described as the sound that you make when you blow your nose.

But the Flying Willybums were so bored with the primitive human species, and found them to be of no interest whatsoever, that they chose to ignore them completely. Thus, the human race was destined to evolve in isolation, and with all the problems that that caused.

Mr P was reading a book, and Gertie was doing some knitting. 'Babe,' she asked, 'have you ever noticed that you have a, kind of, better sense of awareness than I do? But not in the premonition type of way, but just more, well, sort of, aware of stuff? Because I've noticed.'

Mr P carried on reading his book. 'That's because you're new, Gertie,' he answered.

She frowned. 'How do you mean, I'm new?'

Mr P put down his book and took the glasses from off his nose. 'Have you never heard of the term new, or, they've been here before?'

'Have I chuff! What are you on about?' she asked again.

'Well, it's quite simple really, babe. Some of us have been on this mortal plain before. Some, many times before. This is why you will meet Dinglewits that are worldly, and aware of things. It's a bit like having an old head on new shoulders, if you get my drift.'

'Riiiiight.'

'While others are brand new,' he continued, 'these Dinglewits come across as a bit naive sometimes, or over trusting. The new ones that always seem to look for the best in others, or do silly things, or are a just a bit clumsy and ditzy. Perfectly innocent of course, but just funny to others. That sort of thing.'

'So you're saying that I'm brand new?'

'Yes, babe, this is your first time on the block. You are discovering everything for the first time. Everything is a wonder to you. The next time you are here, in probably a hundred years or so, you will see things a little differently. And then, in another hundred years or so, when you are next here, it will be different again.'

'Are you being serious?' she asked. 'I can never tell when you are being serious.'

'Yeah, I'm being deadly serious Gertie. It's a well-known fact that is.' He placed his book on the table next to the chair, and crossed his legs to try and look intellectual.

'So you are honestly saying to me that this is my first time on the mortal coil, and that is why I fall for everything?' Gertie responded.

'Yeah, sort of. It's a great thing though, babe. You should embrace the newness of everything, because next time it won't be as spectacular. Next time it will all be a case of, oh, that again or, yeah, I've seen that before, and things won't seem as splendid as they do this time.' Mr P answered, now trying to reassure her that it is not a bad thing to be a tad gullible at times.

'Oh really,' Gertie snapped back, 'and what, exactly, is so splendid about it all this, this time around, eh?'

Mr P could see that Gertie was getting triggered; he always enjoyed watching Gertie get triggered, because he knew that it nearly always ended in her throwing something at him.

'Well,' he responded, 'splendid, like, err, our relationship, that is splendid to you.'

'Oh, is it really?'

'Yeah. You see, to you, Gertie, our love is the greatest thing ever. You love walking through fields of wild flowers while holding hands. You enjoy our walks on the beach at night as the waves come crashing in against the sand. You look at the clouds in the sky with a wonderment that this must be created by something, because nothing that is this beautiful can happen purely by chance. That sort of thing. Next time around though, it will be like, oh, yeah, they are clouds, nothing special there!'

Gertie curled her toes. Then chucked a ball of wool at him. Mr P smirked, and got back on with his book.

But it was a real shame that the Flying Willybums chose to ignore humans though, because they were a form of siphonophore that had evolved from the crossbreeding of several intergalactic species in the early Holocene era, and as such, had traits that are most agreeable to everyone they meet. First, we have the previously described erotic dancers, which are a feast for the eyes, as witnessed by every lifeform they encounter. And second, and by far their most outstanding feature, is that they possess a highly developed sense of satori — a kind of premonition that allows them to manipulate any situation for their own benefit and profit.

Unbeknown to either of our lead characters in this story, Mr P has some Flying Willybum in him. His great grandmother had engaged in a one-off fling with a mobile carpet salesman, who was really on the run from the authorities for guessing football scores, and so, after three more generations, Mr P was born. This mysterious carpet salesman was, in fact, a Flying Willybum, and so, an element of satori was deep in the genes of our illustrious adventurer.

Because of their uncanny ability to know everything, the Flying Willybums are the unofficial rulers of the universe. But they choose to stay in the background, as some sort of secret society, controlling the, so-called, elected leaders, and making sure that the status quo remains intact.

As is well known, the big problem with dominance without scrutiny, is that those at the top become above all censure, and begin to behave accordingly. This is definitely the case with the Flying Willybums, and the 'hidden hand' has been instrumental in all the wars and conflicts that have ever taken place over the centuries. To this day they are still pulling the strings in order to preserve their secret elevated status.

This was the case if you look into the death of the most famous Flying Willybum, the erotic dancer, Nadia, who was famous for having eleven titties that could behave independently. She was much loved and adored wherever she travelled, and was able to sell this talent to pretty much anyone. And soon became very rich on the revenues.

Her death was a great shock to every nation as no famous Flying Willybum had ever succumbed to an untimely death — due their satori ability I presume — and there was suspicion a plenty.

Mr P was a great admirer of Nadia, and was as shocked as everyone else when the news broke of her apparent accident. And to this day he finds it hard to believe that her hovercraft overturned while trying to evade the paparazzi.

As does everybody else.

The Liberty Coin

Drinking an orange Neptunium potato concoction, that tastes remarkably like pink gin, Mr P and Gertie are sat in their garden. It was bought by Gertie's sister on her way back from her tour of the outer planets a few years earlier, and as yet not had time to ferment properly. This was partly due to the lack of moisture on Neptune since the Rosos tribe invaded the planet and stole its only ocean to sell on the open market, and partly because Neptunium potatoes are well known for being the worst tasting potatoes in the whole universe. The only reason why any species would bother drinking the stuff is because it is rare and expensive, which therefore makes it special and considered a treat. It is often described as an 'acquired taste.'

'It's a bit dull, babe,' said Gertie while looking at the coin given to her by Percival.

Mr P agreed. 'It's a 1933 King George V penny with some sort of heavy thing implanted in the middle of the coin by the look and feel of it,' he replied. 'I've been comparing it to other old coins and there is definitely something in the middle of this coin.'

Gertie seemed perplexed. 'It's just a piece of old brown metal. How is this valuable?'

'Hmm, I dunno. It looks like it's made of base metals, Gertie, so it's not the metal in itself that is valuable. So maybe it's the whole thing, the sum of all its parts,' came the reply from Mr P.

'So we can't melt it down and flog it then?' came the rather unenthusiastic response from Gertie.

'God, no, it's an ancient human coin from before their first world war,' answered Mr P. 'There is more to this coin than meets the eye. I've been doing some research. There were only seven of these coins made and no one knows why. They are immensely valuable!'

Gertie passed the coin to Mr P and said, 'Here, you look after it. I don't want the responsibility.'

Mr P took possession of the coin and walked through the garden and past their daughter, Mya, who was sat near the water feature playing space toads on her phone.

Space toads is an online game where players have to find toads through the depths of space. Generations of youngsters have played varying versions of this pointless time-wasting hogwash of a past time, rather than actually doing something useful or skilful.

As Mr P slowly walked past Mya, she let out a screech, 'Muuuum I have lost signal,' she screamed at the top of her voice.

As Mr P slowly walked a further 2 metres Mya continued, 'It's OK, it's come back now.'

Mr P stopped and turned to look, paused for a few seconds, then slowly walked back towards her.

'Nooooo,' Mya yelped. 'It's gone again.'

Mr P stopped, turned around, and walked away once more. With that Mya shouted out again. 'It's OK, it's back.'

Mr P looked at Mya, looked at the coin. He then looked at Mya again. 'It's this coin,' he said. 'Gertie, come here!'

'Is the coin cutting out the ethernet?' she asked, as she got up from her cushioned swinging chair.

'Yes,' smiled Mr P. 'It is cutting out the signal to a radius of about 2 metres or so.' Mr P looked down at the coin 'It causes about a five-metre blackout wherever we are. They can't see us when we are holding this coin. This is astounding.'

He gripped the coin tight, and placed it against his chest, as if it was the most valuable thing in the world.

'Who can't see us?' Gertie replied.

'Them… they can't see us!' came his response. 'When we have this coin, we are off the radar, babe, we are truly free, they can't monitor us, they can't trace us, we are free to move and do whatever we want without the authorities watching over us. This is brilliant.'

'But why would anyone want to see us, babe? said Gertie.

'It doesn't matter, Gertie,' Mr P ranted. 'We spend our lives constantly in the watch of the man, but when we have this coin, we are free to do whatever we want, and they can't see us. This coin is liberty. This coin is freedom. That's what its true value is.'

Mr P ran into the house and put on his shoes. 'Where are you going?' shouted Gertie.

'I'm going into town! You coming?' said Mr P, now very excited.

Within a few minutes they were both in Logey the campervan and heading into the town centre. They parked up next to the big tree by the Guildhall and Mr P grabbed Gertie by the hand and led her to the shops. Situated on the high street was the technology shop, "Skinners", which displayed a giant circular rotating screen on the outside of the shop that received signals from the CCTV cameras situated across the road.

Mr P and Gertie stood still holding hands and waited for their image to appear on the screen. They waited and waited, but nothing. An elderly Dinglewit wearing a pink coat walked past them, and she appeared on the screen... but not them.

They continued to stand still and wait for their image to appear on the screen, but it never did. They stood and watched as all the Dinglewits that walked along the high street appeared on the screen, but they never did.

They were, to all intents and purposes, *invisible*. The coin makes them invisible to the monitors and cameras and the satellites and the spy-cams that are used to watch over the population.

'We are free, Gertie, while we carry this coin, they can't watch us,' said Mr P with a lump in his throat. 'Percival has given us a small piece of liberty.'

'Wow!' replied Gertie.

They turned and headed back home. They didn't speak. They had nothing to say.

What they did know was that the coin was special and it had given them something that no Dinglewit had experienced in hundreds of years, true liberty.

Now, Mr P and Gertie had nothing to hide, and they certainly aren't about to start being activists, but the thought that they have true privacy for the first time was mind-blowing to them. For the first time there was no one listening to their conversation, no one checking their computer search history, and for the first time they could walk to the shops without being monitored. Just simple little things that were taken for granted centuries earlier when the humans walked the earth but had gradually been taken away due to varying excuses from successive administrations.

'What do you wanna do?' asked Gertie.

Mr P looked lost, his gaze had been unbroken for some time and his jovial spirit currently taking a well-earned break.

'I want to get a burger, with fries, and a side of onions,' Mr P mumbled, 'and then I'm going to visit Cleese!'

Cleese

Cleese was an absolute legend to his friends — and also a wizard. He spent the best part of his youth mixing, experimenting and smoking copious amounts of herbs that he had bred and mixed from plants that he had gathered over the years. His lifetime hobby meant that, at some point, Cleese had bred, crossbred, created, farmed and smoked pretty much every plant in the known universe, but he always preferred Earth plants to any other.

He took pride in creating new species, and he even had his own naming system, as he felt the established one was a bit dreary and dull. As far as he knew he wasn't breaking any laws. He never sold his product. And he never shared his secrets with anyone. So for all tents and purposes, he was a hermit herb smoker living his best. And this way of life basically allowed him to continue with his experiments, creating his own unique flavoured herbs for his own pleasure, and honing his skills as a master craftsman. In fact, while at school, his science teacher was so impressed with his horticultural abilities that they became friends. Good friends. They shared techniques and experiences in order to create the greatest flavours known to Dinglewit, and she was so impressed with the product of Cleese's unique fermentation process, that she acquired the occasional exotic substance from him from time to time.

After Cleese left school they stayed in touch.

Mr P and Cleese first became friends at junior school. They had grown up together and had developed a sixth sense that only true friends can understand. They enjoyed many a childhood evening playing dungeons and dragons and eating plants, much to the dismay of their parents, and they had been inseparable ever since.

Mr P's favourite brand of Cleese's herbal range was a Khao Lak Sativa plant, mixed with a Beqaa Valley Indica cutting, and spliced with Ruderalis to help it grow. They called the plant the "illustrious", because it made you feel immortal. The ingredients were acquired during a trip to Egypt where many various florae can be bought without question. No one else enjoyed it because of its smooth presentation and its sudden urge to flatten you if you exceeded the optimal dose, which was just fine for Mr P, as he didn't much enjoy sharing it anyway.

'Sup P,' said Cleese as Mr P walked up the pathway towards his house on the edge of town.

'My dear dude, I have something to show you,' Mr P replied. 'It's gonna blow your mind.'

'Then enter yourself into my kingdom and explain all,' came the reply.

Cleese looked stoned. He was always under the influence of something of an agricultural nature, and today was no exception. His kingdom consisted of an open plan living and sleeping area with a massive hot tub at the far end near the garden in which all his amazing creations were born. Cleese loved it here, and Mr P was slightly jealous of the hedonistic libertarian nature of his existence.

'I'm seeking the meaning of life, Cleese, and in my journey so far I have acquired this,' said Mr P, as he showed him the coin.

'What's that, my inquisitive brother?' asked Cleese.

'I call it the Liberty Coin, it's awesome, when you have it on your person there is a five-metre area of silicon silence around you, they can't see you. The cameras don't pick you up. No face recognition. No signal from your phone being monitored. No A.I. robot listening in on your conversation. Nothing. You are free,' answered Mr P.

'Wooooord!' commented Cleese 'are you serious?'

'Never been more serious, oh great wizard, and you wouldn't believe how I got hold of it,' said Mr P loosely pointing at Cleese. 'This is a game changer for sure.'

Cleese slowly walked over to Mr P and with his thumb and index finger took possession of the coin. He turned it over a few times and then moved the coin closer to his eyes. 'It's a bit dull, brethren, what's it made from?' Cleese asked.

'Oh, just it's just made up of base metals, but it feels like there is something in the middle of it,' answered Mr P.

'Wow,' stated Cleese, and he held up the coin to the light, 'it's a priceless piece of worthless metal that changes the entire universe,' he continued. Cleese always had a tendency to overstate the obvious, and then make a bold assertion. 'Let's change existence!' he added.

Now Cleese was always a bit dramatic, but on this occasion Mr P was inclined to agree with him. In the right hands this coin was indeed very special, but in the wrong hands it could be very sinister. A responsibility not lost on Mr P or Cleese.

'This is just like the Arc of the Covenant, P, or the Book of Thoth,' Cleese continued. 'It's priceless, have you tested it out?'

'Yeah, me and Gertie went into town earlier, total blackout from all surveillance apparatus, even the cameras could not see us when we stood right in front of them, it's magic, Cleese, simply magic,' replied Mr P.

Cleese handed the coin back to Mr P and then sat on a footstool made from bamboo. For the first time he was genuinely speechless. 'We need a plan,' Cleese murmured.

'A plan! Dude, you don't do plans,' laughed Mr P.

'Not normally I don't, but this... this is different,' Cleese stated.

'Well,' said Mr P, 'I plan to find out the truth. I'm gonna find out what they've been hiding for all these years. I'm gonna find out if we were intended; if we were made, or if we are simply a consequence of random events. I'm gonna seek meaning to it all and the Liberty Coin will help.'

Cleese stood up and walked to the fridge. 'Do you want a drink P?'

'Oh, go then,' came the reply.

And with that they both walked into the garden for a few quiet, and friendly drinks, and the occasional indulgence in herbal therapy.

Hours passed, conversations came and went, plans were discussed, and drinks were consumed. Eventually Mr P staggered to his feet, and with a whisp in his voice, said, 'I will run it by Gertie.' And with that he gingerly walked out of the garden and headed back home.

Cleese remained sat in his chair for several hours trying to ponder the consequences of what this coin can have. His days of observation may soon be over and he will finally be free to pursue unlimited freedom that no Dinglewit had ever been given before.

He then fell asleep due to all the toxins he had ingested.

The Crumpet Theory

Gertie had just got out of the bath and was chilling in the lounge when Mr P arrived home from his meeting with Cleese. She seemed to understand that some sort of decision had been made, and more than likely, a hair brained plan formulated, but as yet, she couldn't care less what it was. She had lesser things to think about, things much less exciting than changing the universe, but a damn site more fun.

There was nothing worth watching on the hologram set, so she sat listening to the radio. It was funky hour, and an old song from the human era was playing. Gertie liked ancient human music; it was much better than the modern Dinglewit noise that was passing as music nowadays. So there she was, enjoying a few peaceful hours when Mr P interrupted her bliss.

'Babe?' he said, as he walked into the hallway, 'I have a suggestion.'

Now Gertie knew better than to just accept every idea that Mr P came up with, and so carried on with her business without giving too much attention.

'We are going to the Isle of Avalon Port!' he announced.

'No, we are not,' replied Gertie. 'I don't know what you two have been talking about, but we are not going to a military restricted area.'

Now, the Isle of Avalon is just what Gertie said it was, a secret military establishment in the middle of nowhere where very few Dinglewits know of its actions. Some claim it was the spaceport where species from other planets in the universe first made contact with the previously endogenous human race. Others say that it is an area where future weapons of war are designed and built. Most Dinglewits know that it is restricted and anyone trying to get in can be in big trouble. Mr P had a book on the Isle of Avalon and understood perfectly the amount of surveillance around the area, but with the Liberty Coin he may be able to get close or even in.

'That is a very bad idea, babe, you can get into big, big, trouble!' Gertie continued. 'WE, Gertie, WE could get into trouble,' replied Mr P 'I ain't doing it without you.'

'Oh, nooo, why do you want to go to the Isle of Avalon, babe? There is nothing there except military people doing military stuff. That is nothing we want to be involved in,' asked Gertie.

By now she had stopped brushing her hair and was sitting uncomfortably on a sofa.

'Because I think they know stuff, babe, and they are keeping it from us,' Mr P explained.

It's not been previously mentioned, but may seem obvious to any astute reader, but Mr P is a massive conspiracy theorist, and his number one theory of all theories is the Crumpet Theory. The crux of the Crumpet Theory is that the universe is a big circle consisting of wormholes of time that allow for movement between each layer of existence — just like a crumpet. It's not ball shaped, it's flat(ish) and due to the spinning nature of particles it could potentially look like a crumpet.

Now the Crumpet Theory loosely aligns itself with Einstein's general relativity, to the extent, that the curvature of space and time relies on the body mass of planets, but does not believe that the universe is spherical. The relative compression of the universe, as stated in the Crumpet Theory, is as a result of dynamic spin, and the thickness of the universe is due to magnetic repulsion. This made much more sense to Mr P than all the other theories that are currently doing the rounds.

'I think there's a wormhole in there, Gertie,' Mr P claimed in an excited mood, 'that's why it is so closely guarded. A wormhole, babe! Just imagine that. Just imagine if we could go into a wormhole. Just imagine all the new discoveries we could find. All the new experiences. It would be fantastic. And this coin will get us inside we reckon,' he continued.

'We?' Gertie responded. 'Let me guess. Cleese! Eh! Cleese has convinced you that trespassing on a military base is OK, hasn't he?'

'Errm, well, it was more of a joint decision.'

'Joint being the word,' answered Gertie. 'He has spent his life making joint decisions, and when I say joint, I don't mean with other Dinglewits. No, this is a bad idea, really bad.'

'But we could find the truth to the universe, babe. We could prove or disprove the theories of the universe, and all that stuff.'

'All that stuff! Oh no,' Gertie had just cottoned on. 'Is this all to do with your Crumpet Theory? Because if it is, are you really going to risk your life because of it?'

Mr P paused, sat down and thought for a while. 'Babe,' Mr P said, 'in order to understand meaning, we must need know the truth, and in the Isle of Avalon there is some truth. Oh, and by the way… we are getting the band back together.'

Gertie was less than impressed.

The Band

The following morning Geoffrey and Cleese turned up at the house, with backpacks in situ, and a smile on both faces. Gertie answered the door. 'And what do you two reprobates want?' she asked knowingly.

'Aye up, Gertie,' answered Geoffrey. 'Is he in? We got the band back together!'

Now Gertie knew what this meant. You see, the band had nothing to do with music. It was an adventure band. A group of friends who got together to do stuff, and they called themselves the LPMD.

The LPMD were a tribe of silly, reckless Dinglewits, thought Gertie, that got together to do adventurous things like, climb high mountains for no reason, go on treasure hunting expeditions, perform dares, to travel to obscure far flung planets and instantly regret it, and buy old motor vehicles to be pimped up and sold for profit, that sort of thing, and now they were going on an adventure to the Isle of Avalon to find a wormhole in time.

Gertie smiled. 'Well boys, this trio have just become a quartet, I'm now in the band too!'

'Really?' asked Cleese, 'is that wise, Gertie, you know how much you dislike our adventures?'

'Yes, it is very wise, Cleese,' she answered. 'Bog-snorkling for gold is one thing, but I'm not about to let you take my man to a military base to be killed. Not without me anyway.'

Cleese looked at Geoffrey, who looked back at Cleese, they shrugged their shoulders, and with a quick pause gave out a cheer.

'Well, OK then,' stated Cleese, 'the new LPMD is formed.' And they high fived each other.

'Oh wait,' snapped Cleese, 'we are gonna need a new flag then!'

'Why's that?' answered Gertie.

'Because it's a boys' club, it's always been a boys' club. And now we have a girl. We might even need a new name as well,' claimed Cleese as he put down his backpack and walked over to the fridge to look for food.

'Yeah, and a new theme tune,' added Geoffrey.

'And a new t-shirt!' shouted Mr P as he was walking down the stairs.

'Why a new name?' asked Gertie.

Mr P Cleese and Geoffrey stood still, looking at each other. They all shook their heads.

It was pretty obvious to Gertie that she wasn't about to find out what LPMD stood for, and if truth were told, she didn't really care about their secrets name anyway. She was too pre-occupied in trying to keep them all alive, on what was obviously, a very dangerous adventure.

'Is everyone ready?' she asked, 'then let's go!'

Geoffrey and the Terminator

The quartet travelled to the Isle of Avalon Port in a convoy. Gertie and Mr P travelled in Logey the campervan, and Geoffrey and Cleese travelled down in Geoffrey's pimped up car that he called the Terminator — presumably because it's black and with a skull and crossbones on the bonnet. Geoffrey bought the Terminator from a dodgy second-hand car salesman from Mars, but it is the best car he ever owned, and as a result, the two are inseparable. He drove to his wedding in it, he spent more money on it than he did his wife and house combined, and he slept in it during his divorce. To this day they are known as Geoffrey and the Terminator.

And so, with bags packed, and nourishment sorted, they headed off for the long journey to the middle of nowhere to seek a wormhole.

They arrived at the Isle just as dusk approached. Mr P and Gertie arrived first and set up camp about half a mile from the base. They chose to camp behind a giant rock that was a completely different colour to the others and must have been transported there at some point. But from that vantage point, they could see the military base lights, and the main road that leads into it. Surrounding the base are apple trees, thousands of them. The trees are well established too, they had clearly been there for many, many, years. And the apples tasted very sweet indeed. Gertie had to tell Mr P to stop picking them in fear of being seen.

They had been there for about an hour before Cleese and Geoffrey and the Terminator arrived, by which time, they had taken note of the comings and goings of the military personnel. As well as feasted on way too many apples.

'How you doing guys?' asked Cleese as he arrived at the giant rock.

'I've been watching the base,' replied Mr P. 'It's a hive of activity, it is going to be difficult to get in I reckon.'

'Well let's get set up and have a rethink,' answered Cleese.

At this point Gertie started began to walk towards the base. She walked about twenty metres then stopped. 'I think there is another way in,' she said. 'I have been watching some cars go in, there seems to be an unofficial entrance over to the right-hand side.'

'That's probably our best shout I think,' continued Mr P. 'Let's go check it out, because if they find out we are here, they will move us on. And I wanna have a go at getting inside.'

'Or at the very least they will keep an eye on us,' chirped in Geoffrey.

'Hang on,' interrupted Cleese, 'do you know what today is?'

'Er no,' answered the rest of the New LPMD in unison.

'It's Friday the 17th, we can't do anything on Friday 17th,' he answered. 'We need to wait until tomorrow.'

Now Cleese was of Italian heritage and Friday 17th is a very unlucky day for them because it is written as XVII which is very close to XIVI that means "I have lived" and implies death in the present. Cleese was very superstitious.

'Dude,' interjected Mr P, 'there is no way we can just sit here until tomorrow, they will see us.'

'Well what time is it?' asked Cleese.

'It's about ten o'clock brother,' said Geoffrey.

'OK just promise me that we don't anything until after midnight,' added Cleese. They all looked at each other.

'OK, deal,' said Gertie not wanting to be left out of any decisions that could potentially get her killed. 'We can take a look and make a plan but not do anything until after midnight.'

'Sounds like a plan to me,' added Geoffrey.

They agreed, and with that they hid away all their belongings inside Logey the campervan and the Terminator and started to gingerly walk around to the right side of the base.

The approach was quite steep and the four intrepid explorers had separated somewhat by the time they approached the side gate. Cleese was trailing behind at the back with Geoffrey not far in front of him; just Mr P and Gertie had managed to stay close together. All of a sudden, a beam of light shone from the top of one of the towers that were guarding the perimeter and beamed directly at Cleese and Geoffrey. They were instantly startled, stood motionless for a few seconds then turned and ran back up the hill. Gertie put her arms around Mr P and they both crouched, in open view, near the gate.

They could see movement from within the compound, which then turned into moving bodies, which then turned into running bodies. More lights came on and within a few seconds the whole area was lit up, Mr P and Gertie were in plain sight. Four military personnel rushed through the gate and headed towards, the now retreating, Cleese and Geoffrey but after a few metres they stopped, as it was obvious that the two intruders had run away. Mr P and Gertie slowly stood up and looked directly at the four guards, but the guards did not seem to notice them, in fact, the guards could not see them at all. The four guards stood for a short time looking around making sure that the threat had gone, then began to walk back to the gate. As they were walking Gertie noticed that their gait was not one of a normal Dinglewit, she squinted her eyes, and her suspicions became aroused.

'They can't see us,' she whispered. 'They can't see us because they are robots.' Mr P looked at Gertie, and then back at the robotic guards.

'Do you have the Liberty Coin?' she asked.

'Yes,' replied Mr P, and with that he put his hand in his pocket and pulled out the coin. 'We are invisible to them,' he whispered, 'the coin is rendering us invisible. I think we are in business, babe.'

'Yes, let's get closer and chance our luck.'

Mr P shook his head in disbelief. 'Bloody hell, Gertie, you go from one extreme to the other.'

'But it's exciting innit,' she answered. 'Come on slow coach. The robot guards are heading back inside.'

'What? Do you want to go inside now?' he asked.

'Yeah, let's see if we can get in the building and take a look around.'

'Bloody hell, Gertie. OK then. Let's do it.'

There was a silence for a few seconds while they allowed the implications of trespassing on a secret military base to sink in, then, without a second for pause, they steadfastly walked through the gate and up to the building door, where they waited for the robotic guards to join them.

This seemed to take forever.

'They don't rush around, do they?' asked Gertie in a hushed tone.

'I bet they can move when they need to though,' Mr P answered.

'Well, maybe, but they can't see us, so we're OK.'

'This is true. OK quiet, they are coming.'

The robots arrived back at the building in single file.

The building door had a lock that needed a number to open it, and as the robots approached the door, the first guard tapped in the number 9781916025806. Gertie had pre-empted this being a ridiculously long number — being as they were robots and could remember long numbers — and so recorded it on her phone.

Mr P gave her the thumbs up.

The robots entered the building and the door closed.

They waited for a few minutes, dialled in the numbers, and cautiously entered the building.

The importance of being a sea squirt

The sea squirt is a member of the phylum chordata that, rather surprisingly, is in the same group as humans — although one could never acquire this information simply by their appearance. The sea squirt begins its life in a fish-like manner with a spinal cord and a brain that it uses to navigate around the ocean looking for a suitable place to settle. What distinguishes the sea squirt from most other living creatures is that it will undergo a transformation, not unlike, at least in metaphorical terms anyway, that of Dinglewits (and some would say humans too), in that once it finds a comfortable place to live, many of the advanced features will disappear, or to be more precise, the brain disappears.

Thus, once the sea squirt finds a suitable habitat, it no longer requires the need to think and move, and will merely exist in its comfortable state until death. In short, the sea squirt eats its own brain. In biological terms the sea squirt feels that it no longer needs a brain to exist, and so absorbs it. According to nature's rules this is a very efficient way to live. Of course once the brain has been eaten it cannot be remade — it is literally a decision made for life and cannot be changed. Thus, while the sea squirt is moving it needs a brain, but once it stops, it doesn't.

On this occasion Cleese and Geoffrey could definitely not be labelled as sea squirts because they were moving, and really moving. They ran back up the hill and headed towards the rock from which they started. As they arrived, now out of breath, Cleese grasped Geoffrey by the collar. 'I told you it was unlucky,' he said in an exhausted voice.

'Well, we'll stay here until they return,' answered Geoffrey.

'It's Friday 17th and Friday 17th is bad luck, I'm staying here,' Cleese replied.

And with that they sat down. And they had every intention of staying sat down.

Inside the military building the lights were dim, and there was very little sound. The rumblings of a generator broke the silence, and the rumblings seemed to vibrate off the metal flooring and echo all around the gigantic room.

Gertie looked at Mr P. 'What do you wanna do now, babe?' she asked.

'We find the wormhole machine,' came the reply.

'The wormhole machine? I'm pretty sure it's not called that y'know,' Gertie answered sarcastically.

'No, probably not. But it would be if I had invented it.'

Mr P stood still and gazed around the room looking for any sign that might point him in the right direction.

'Let's go… err… right,' he said.

Neither knew whether going left or going right was correct. So going right seemed as good a decision as going left. So they walked to the right.

The building was empty of all life, and it seemed like they had the place to themselves.

Gertie grabbed Mr P's hand to make him stop. 'We need to be careful of lifeforms, babe, the robots can't see us, but Dinglewits can,' she said in a quiet and nervous tone.

'Agreed,' came the reply. 'Let's keep going.'

They walked through another door that led to a corridor. They followed it round until they were confronted by another door with a sign on it. It read:

"Restricted access. Wormhole machine inside. Authorised personnel only"

'This is it, Gertie, this is the where the wormhole machine is kept.' And without a second to waste he opened the door.

Gertie looked at the door that said, wormhole machine inside, and she shook her head in bewilderment. 'It is called a "wormhole machine" after all, she thought. Dinglewit men are so unimaginative.

Inside was a cylindrical machine with flashing lights on it. The top half of the machine was rotating clockwise and the bottom half was still and contained an entrance. To the left of the machine stood two robots pressing buttons and moving handles. They were paying no attention to Mr P and Gertie and just carried on doing their chores, while seemingly not noticing them. This made it easy to walk over to the wormhole machine where they noticed that inside the entrance was a reflective liquid.

'You see this in films, Gertie,' said Mr P. 'If you walk through the liquid you will go to another dimension in time.'

'Eh?'

'Yeah, let's just jump through it!'

'Knickers to that!' Gertie replied.

'Why? What's up?'

'Well, what if we don't just jump into another dimension,' replied Gertie. 'What if it's just an energy machine, and if we are just jumping to our deaths.'

'Oh, don't be a wuss, come on.'

They held hands, and with barely a pause for thought, they both jumped through the reflective liquid.

Squish!

Frisby

On the other side of the liquid, and inside the wormhole machine, there did not seem to be an atmosphere. Mr P and Gertie felt weightless as if they were in space casually drifting around. There was no perception of time, no sensation of gravity, and definitely no emotion. They just existed, floating around in a soulless atmosphere.

Are we dead? Gertie thought to herself. Was it an energy field that they had jumped into and now they are in purgatory? Had they made a massive mistake, and are now dead?

A few more timeless seconds went by when, suddenly, and without warning, a very bright light appeared to their right-hand side. Gertie stretched out her hand towards the light and in a flash, they were both vacuumed straight through it.

The next thing they realised, they were both standing in a room very similar, in fact, the same as the room they had just left. The only problem though is that they couldn't see very well. It was as if their eyes didn't work as well as they used to. Everything seemed red and the air was sort of moving in waves, flowing back and forth, and in a clockwise spiral.

Gertie turned to Mr P. 'Babe, I'm scared, what has happened?'

'I dunno, Gertie, what is your vision like?'

'Everything is red and blurry.'

'Yeah, same here, let's just give it a few seconds.'

They held hands trying to comfort each other. But they needn't have been scared, because within a few seconds the redness began to ease, and the normal colour of things returned.

They looked around, and saw that the walls were the same. The stairs were the same. And the lights were the same. But then, considering that it was all made of metal, it was hardly surprising.

The gravity of their surroundings felt familiar, and the air that they breathed felt exactly the same — maybe even fresher. They were still on Earth, and they both knew it. Gertie began to walk around to the other side of the machine where she saw a control panel with a row of flashing lights and a dial that controlled a digital calendar. On top of the control panel was a digital clock that read:

14:16

Wednesday

22nd February 2033

She touched the panel with the tip of her fingers, as if drawn to do so, but without a reason why. Gertie liked to touch things that she found interesting; it gave her a sense of reality.

'Babe,' she said, 'I think we have travelled back in time, back to 2033.'

Mr P did not seem too surprised by this fact. He slowly walked to the side of the machine where she was stood transfixed to the control panel and took hold of her hand. 'OK, 2033. So the rumours were right all along,' he answered.

'Rumours? What rumours?'

Mr P felt that he needed to explain. 'Well,' he started, 'there was a rumour that in 2033, human time, the world that they lived in changed. It was like a day of reckoning. The A.I. technology took over the day-to-day chores, and humans were side-lined from work.'

'Oh, well that doesn't sound too bad,' Gertie answered.

'No, but the reality was very different. It was the start of the end for the human way of life. A similar thing happened to the Battenburgs on planet Gliesse 442, and it only ended following an apocalyptic war. But the humans never recovered from what I hear. That's probably why they were so keen to leave the planet when they did.'

'Oh,' Gertie answered. 'Well, they were a strange species.' But they both knew the gravity of this situation.

They couldn't just walk about, because in this time zone they are aliens from outer space that humans are yet to encounter. If human eyes see them, they could be in big trouble. And they both knew it.

They both, so desperately, wanted to explore, but it wouldn't be safe, and they might never be allowed to go back if they were found. So for the next few moments they stood still and looked around for anything of interest.

But then Mr P smiled. 'So time travel is possible,' he said, in a happy tone, 'but yet, nobody really knows. Only us.'

'Well, some do,' replied Gertie.

'I will bet you that some do.'

Mr P thought for a while.

'Yeah, I think you are right, but what else aren't they telling us?'

Gertie gave a sigh. 'Let's go home.'

'Yeah, let's get outta here,' Mr P replied. He led Gertie by the hand, and they both walked to the exit.

'Wait, stop,' shouted Gertie. 'We need to change the time on the machine or we will just come back here to the same place.'

'Yeah, good point. Wait. No,' replied Mr P. 'I think it's the coin that is deciding where we go. Don't ask me how I know this, but I think each coin offers a different time for transportation. This one must allow for travel between 2033 and our present time. Trust me, babe, I think I'm right on this.'

For some strange reason this seemed to make sense, and they both nodded in agreement.

'Oh gosh,' said Gertie, 'what is going on in the universe? This is so weird.'

'I think there is more going on than we will ever find out, babe. And this shows it. I bet there are Dinglewits, and probably humans, that knew about time travel y'know, but they kept it to themselves.'

'Why would they do that?'

'Because knowledge is power, that's why. Come on, let's get out of here.'

In a coordinated action they took a one last glimpse around, and simultaneously jumped back into the time machine.

As before, they drifted in weightlessness for a few seconds before an entrance appeared. And as before, with an outstretched arm Mr P grasped for the entrance, and they both flew through the liquid and back to where they started.

'Well, this is fun, babe,' commented Gertie. 'Are we are back where we started?'

But as before everything seemed red and fuzzy, which took a few seconds to improve, only this time there was a problem. Once the red mist disappeared, they were stood in front of an official looking person with a robot guard on either side. He was wearing a long white doctor's apron, and the robots had guns pointing straight at them.

'Who are you and why are you here?' said the official person with a doctor's apron on.

'My name is Mr P and I'm a time traveller,' said Mr P, with a very large, proud grin on his face. How cool was that to say he thought.

A gazed look appeared on the face of the official person with a doctor's apron on. 'Well, err, how was it?' he said.

'Don't you know?' Mr P replied. Now with an even bigger grin.

'No,' he said. 'No one does, no one has been through it and come back, we have lost two good people trying, so now we just monitor it for activity. Where are you from?'

Mr P and Gertie looked at each other. 'Well hopefully we are from here,' said Gertie. 'Where is here?' she continued.

'This is Earth. Sorry allow me to introduce myself, my name is Frisby, I'm a doctor here at the institute.'

'My name is Gertie what year is it?

'What year do you think it is?' replied Frisby.

'Now don't be coy, Frisby,' added Gertie

'It's 3020?' answered Frisby, 'does that work for you?'

'Yes,' answered Gertie. 'Is it Friday 17th?'

'Yes.'

'Good, we are back to where we started, are we allowed to leave?' asked Gertie.

'Of course, it's not a prison, but would you do me the honour of telling me your experiences first?' asked Frisby. 'My office is just through here,' pointing his finger at a wooden door a few metres away. 'I have coffee.'

Gertie looked at Mr P for guidance on this matter. She had clearly been shaken up by the whole experience and was unsure of Frisby. She was always untrusting of others at first glance, and her instincts were to say no and leave, but Mr P was not so timid.

'Of course, why not?' said Mr P. 'I could do with a coffee.'

'Fantastic, it's this way,' said a now very excited Frisby, and with that they all walked into the office.

When Frisby said that 'he had coffee' he was not lying. There was a 10-foot table along the back wall and on it must have been a hundred different blends of coffee. 'Wow,' said Mr P, 'look at all these different coffees babe.' Pointing at the table.

Gertie began to relax.

They walked over to the table and began picking up the jars one at a time, and looking at the labels.

Frisby looked amused at their enthusiasm. 'These coffees are from all over the universe,' he added. He picked up a green jar with a flower growing from the top. 'This is from the planet Tau Ceti e, it's only ripe for picking one month in every five years. It's the rarest coffee in the universe, but unfortunately not very nice so is cheap, but if you like it like I do it's priceless.'

Frisby handed the jar to Gertie. 'No thanks,' she said handing the jar back. 'I'm more of a tea drinker.'

'That's a shame, what about this one, it's from Earth, it's called Jamaican blue-mountain.'

Mr P took hold of the jar. 'Don't mind if I do,' he said. 'I have tasted this one before, it is exquisite.'

Frisby took the jar and walked over to the cups and began making Mr P a coffee. 'So what did you see while inside the machine?' he asked.

'Well, not a lot,' answered Mr P. 'It was like the world was in infra-red, we could not make out anything.'

'Really?' said Frisby. 'Now that is interesting because there is a theory that if you move into another dimension then the light waves change frequency.'

'How do you mean?' asked Gertie.

'Well, the spectrum of light is vast and we only see a small proportion of it, about 0.0035% to be more exact. Our eyes have adapted to see our part of the universe but not all of it. That means that over 99% of light we cannot see, and some philosophers believe that these light forms are from different dimensions that spill over into ours.'

'So there could be life forms in other dimensions that can see and exist in these different waves of light?' asked Mr P.

'Oh, almost definitely,' replied Frisby, 'in fact I would say that it's a certainty. There are enough personal accounts of out-of-body experiences or Dinglewits being brought back from a dead state to justify this.'

Gertie thought she would find out some answers for herself. Seeing as Mr P was now pre-occupied with coffee. She despaired with him sometimes.

'So do you believe in a multiexistential state, or is it actual different dimensions with different types of matter behaving independently?' she asked.

'I wouldn't say that matter exists in the format that we see in our dimension,' continued Frisby, 'but certainly energy waves exist, and these energy structures can form complex organisations that may think and act independently.'

Mr P looked up from his coffee digression for a second. 'So where does time fit in to this theory, is dark energy or dark matter involved in the fabric of space-time?'

Frisby smiled at Mr P and Gertie. He had had these same thoughts and conversations before, but nothing had been solved.

'Well, we don't know for sure but you being here now having been in the machine shows us that something is out there.'

Mr P didn't wish to give away the secret of the Liberty Coin and the fact that it was probably the coin that holds the key to time travel. He felt like he was cheating this lovely amiable chap who had been nothing but nice to them, especially considering the circumstances, but still could not muster up the integrity to inform him.

Frisby handed a cup of Jamaican blue-mountain coffee to Mr P.

'What about wormholes? Is the machine a wormhole Frisby?' asked Mr P, now feeling very guilty, and wanting to change the subject to something less guilt-ridden.

'I suppose it could be considered a wormhole, especially now,' answered Frisby.

'Where was it made?' asked Gertie.

'We found it so no one knows, what we do know is that it wasn't made by Dinglewits, because it was found on Earth way before we came here.'

'Wow,' said Mr P, 'how old?'

Frisby shrugged his shoulders. 'We think about 3000 BC human time, there is another one in Egypt.'

'I have a theory,' said Mr P. 'I call it the Crumpet Theory.'

He then took a seat on the edge of the table where all the coffee was being kept and continued. Gertie closed her eyes in embarrassment.

'I imagine time to be a bit like a crumpet, where there are different layers or dimensions, and these are connected with holes that I call wormholes, and you move between each layer of dimension. What do you think?' Mr P asked.

Frisby looked at Mr P. 'Again, it's possible but we simply do not know, but by going by your experiences in the machine, it appears that we cannot function very well in other dimensions, but for sure we are going to keep trying.'

'Why?' asked Gertie.

Mr P stood up from the table that he was sitting on and without a pause for thought said, 'I know why, Gertie. To make sense of our existence, to find out why we are here and if we have a purpose.'

Frisby smiled and nodded his head.

Mr P handed the coffee cup back to Frisby. 'Thank you for the coffee, sir, I would like to leave now?' he said.

'Of course,' replied Frisby.

And with that they slowly walked out of the office, past the wormhole machine, back along the corridor and out of the door.

They never spoke a word while walking out, as if the events of the last half hour had overpowered them mute. But as they walked through the door, Mr P stopped, turned, held out his hand and offered it to Frisby. 'Goodbye, Frisby, and good luck with your endeavours.'

'The same to you, Mr P, and good luck with your adventures,' he replied, 'and if you find out anything please come and see me. I will be here and you are most welcome to come anytime.'

And with that final exchange they all turned their separate ways and walked away.

They walked back up the hill following their own footsteps in silence , and as Mr P approached the rock where Cleese and Geoffrey were hiding, he stopped and pulled his notebook and green crayon out of his pocket and wrote:

The meaning of life — 5) Be open-minded

Making deals and cups of teas

Gertie was beginning to look worried. 'Babe, are we going to be OK?' she asked.

'Yes, I think so,' Mr P replied, 'but I don't think life will ever be the same again.'

They got to the rock and peeped over to look at where Geoffrey and Cleese were sitting. 'Guys you will not believe what happened to us,' said Mr P in a self-satisfied tone.

'You went into another time dimension,' answered Geoffrey.

'Eh, how'd you know?' interrupted Gertie.

'HE told us,' chirped in Cleese pointing at a man standing near the top of the hill.

'His name is Ivan and he wants to speak with you both,' said Geoffrey.

In the distance was a silhouette of a male figure wearing a black hat and a long dark coat. He was not very tall, and even though he is wearing some strange attire, he does portray an imposing figure. Slowly they all walked over to Ivan, who was looking slightly nervous by this stage, but in a calm and assured tone he introduced himself. 'Oh, oh, hi guys, my name is Ivan,' came a high-pitched voice. 'I work for the council of the seven seals, I'm very pleased to meet you.'

Ivan then offered his hand of which Mr P happily took.

Mr P turned and looked at Gertie. 'The council of the seven seals, what is that?' he asked, directing the question at Ivan.

'P-p-p-please don't be afraid, um, we are a friendly bunch really, we just want to help,' answered Ivan. 'Can we take a seat? I could do with a drink.'

'Me too,' said Gertie.

'Yes, it's thirsty work travelling through time, isn't it?' continued Ivan. 'I will never get used to it. They say it's because the different energy levels sap water from your body leaving you dehydrated, but it's never been proven. I always try to drink plenty before I jump time dimensions.'

And they sat down near Logey the campervan and made a cup of tea.

'So how many jumps have you done?' asked Gertie.

'Oh loads, yeah, loads,' came the despondent reply, 'I don't enjoy it really, but it's a part of the job you see.'

Mr P began to smile in disbelief, and looked at the other members of the LPMD for a reaction.

'You don't like time travel? Dude, it's ace,' stated Mr P. 'So why are you here, Ivan?'

'Well, just to make contact and chat to you really.'

'Oh.'

'But also, to make you an offer for the coin,' Ivan chipped in.

'An offer?' asked Gertie, 'for the coin? How much?'

Ivan took a sip on his tea and clasped both hands around the cup. 'Well, let me begin with a history lesson into how these coins came into existence.' They all nodded their heads.

'In 1933 humans inhabited the Earth, and here in England the king at the time was King George V. Now this isn't common knowledge but King George was a time traveller, and he travelled into the future and foresaw events well beyond his years. He wrote all his travels down in a diary that has now since been lost. Now on his travels he met with a scientist called Dr Leo Napah who explained that there are seven dimensions in existence and that each dimension has a particular wave cycle. He also gave him instructions on how to access each dimension safely, and this came in the form of an energy wave that could be contained in a metal structure. King George took these energy forms and put them inside seven coins, and these coins are the King George V pennies of which only seven were pressed — one for each dimension. We believe that you may have one of these coins, are we correct?'

Mr P reached in his pocket and took the coin out. He looked at it then handed it to Ivan. 'I've been calling it the Liberty Coin, and it's an amazing thing.'

'It certainly is,' answered Ivan. 'We have four already and this is number five.'

He passed the coin back to Mr P. 'Would you be interested in selling it?' he asked.

Mr P looked around. 'Well, what can you do there, it's full of humans. There is no way we can walk around or blend in,' explained Mr P.

'No, there is more to explore,' added Ivan, 'you see if you have a coin then you can walk around with invisibility.'

'Eh?' chirped in Gertie.

Ivan continued, 'The coin makes you invisible... it's because you are there on a different time dimension. You can walk around amongst them, you can even touch them in a light way, but they can't see you, the dimensions are different you see.'

Mr P and Gertie were clearly on the same page when they heard this from Ivan. They both believe in a spirit world, of some sort, and they both believe that there is more to life, and death, than we are being told. For them there have been far too many sightings and experiences to be simply explained with science and sheer ignorance.

'So if we had just walked around, then we wouldn't have been seen,' added Mr P.

'Yes,' added Ivan, 'and we believe that there are seven such coins, all pinpointing a moment in time.

'Why only seven?' added Cleese, wanting to be a part of the conversation without really understanding the meaning of it.

Ivan continued. 'We believe that there have been seven significant events in the history of this planet. And this can, sort of, be proven with giant leaps in knowledge and skills way beyond what should have happened in that moment. When the Earth was given Isaac Newton for example, he was way ahead of anyone else alive at that time. And he moved science forward to a level that no one else could ever have done. It is extraordinary that he knew so much and could work out the stuff that he did. But many now believe that he had help from future generations, and perhaps a species that was alien to Earth at that time.'

'Wow,' said Mr P. 'I do hope that that is true.'

'Why?' asked Geoffrey.

'Because it would be so cool, so cool to know that there is a circle to it all, and that we are all just the same really.' Ivan burst Mr P's bubble.

'But there is a BUT I'm afraid. With this coin comes responsibility and perhaps some danger.'

This got the attention of the LPMD and they all stopped their mindless playing around, and began to pay very close attention. Ivan continued.

'You see there are some species that would like to have these coins in their possession, and probably have the sixth and seventh one already. We thought they had your fifth coin already if we are honest, and that the history of the human race could well have been manipulated to suit their own means.'

'Ohhhh this is heavy stuff,' chirped in Cleese. 'I think I need a smoke.'

'ME TOO!' added Geoffrey, and with that the two walked over to a grassy mound and sat down.

'Do you think you will sell us the coin?' Ivan asked Mr P.

'Yeah probably,' he answered. 'I do want to find the meaning to life but I'm also skint, I'm sure we can come to a deal. Have you met Frisby by the way?'

'Oh, yes, I knew him years ago, we trained together, he was top of the class. He chose to go into a laboratory whereas I went into business. He works here, doesn't he?' asked Ivan.

'You need to speak with him, and tell him all about this stuff, he's good people y'know.'

'Yes, I will,' came the assurance. 'Now, about this coin you have?'

Do you fear Phobophobia?

On this particular Sunday morning, as Mr P and Geoffrey walked down to the local shop to get a newspaper, there was no real weather to speak of. There was no wind, no noticeable temperature, and the sun wasn't too bright or too dull. It was almost as if their Earth was in a vacuum.

'Did you know that phobophobia is the fear of fear?' asked Mr P. 'Don't you think it's kinda strange that there is a fear of fear?'

'Aye,' answered Geoffrey. 'You wouldn't think that you could fear fear, because that's a sort of self-induced positive feedback loop, and you would think that the brain would have found a way to prevent it. Or is it a negative feedback loop?

'No definitely a positive one.'

Mr P agreed. 'Yeah, definitely a positive feedback loop because it amplifies a reaction, but anyway there are loads of phobias, I've been reading up on it, for example did you know that achondroplasiaphobia is a fear of midgets? Now how can you be afraid of midgets, surely a phobia has to be rational, a meaningful threat to life and what threat to life are midgets? It makes no sense if you ask me.'

'I knew a girl who was afraid of kissing,' added Geoffrey. 'I think it's called philematophobia, her boyfriend was well pissed off.'

'Well as long as she wasn't phallophobic eh,' added Mr P. They both laughed, clearly neither were geliophobic.

Now Mr P wasn't afraid of clocks or watches as chronomentrophobics are, but he did suffer from slight chronophobia, which is the fear of time passing. He was well aware that time on this mortal coil is limited and that we have to make the most of every minute.

The laughter was soon interrupted by Mr P. 'You know Gertie is afraid of being buried, it's called taphephobia but she isn't afraid of dying.'

'Thanatophobia,' jumped in Geoffrey.

'That would be more rational, as dying is a real-life event, while being buried once dead is meaningless, so should not be a phobia,' explained Mr P.

'What about being buried alive?'

'Ahh subterraneapremortephobia, now that is rational,' answered Mr P.

Geoffrey paused for a second. 'I think that all fears originate in the amygdala and therefore any emotion has the potential of being a phobia,' he said. 'It could be a fear of needles, as in trypanophobia or a fear of the colour purple, as in porphyrophobia, but a phobia should not be an actual thing that does not spark an emotion.'

'Like what?' asked Mr P.

'Liiiiike a number,' answered Geoffrey, 'but there is, there are loads of phobias to numbers, there is a phobia to the number 100, now why is there a phobia to the number 100?'

'My favourite is the name for a phobia of the number 666, it's hexakosioihexekontahexaphobia, which is a very silly word when considering that 666 depicts the devil and a fear of the devil doesn't actually have a name,' answered Mr P.

'This is true, dude, but perhaps it also explains our fear of numbers as well, mathematics is difficult and in the olden days very few could work with numbers, so maybe that's where it comes from,' continued Geoffrey.

'Well, if that is the case,' argued Mr P, 'then how come there is a phobia of the number 999 called enniakosioenenekontenneaphobia. 999 isn't an ancient number, and yet some Dinglewits fear it.'

'Well they are just silly,' came the rather bemused reply.

The local shop that morning was not particularly busy and on sale was a local newspaper that was trying to lure in more readers by reducing its price. It never really works however, but I suppose the advertisers like it. Geoffrey bought a copy of his monthly magazine because he is trying to build an old-fashioned star ship called the "Victory Gin" that became the first star ship to travel to a different solar system with paying customers. It was a triumph of engineering at the time but is now an old relic.

As they left the shop to walk back home the conversation of phobias continued. 'One of the longest words in the dictionary is hippopoto-monstrosequippedaliophobia, which describes a fear of long words rather ironically,' Mr P began, 'but some think that that is a made-up word because sesquipedalophobia also means a fear of long words, but I prefer hippopotomonstrosequippedaliophobia personally.'

'Yeah, that is a superb word,' chipped in Geoffrey. 'I wonder if anyone has been diagnosed with it because I can't imagine any doctor being able to spell it?'

'Yeah, well I'm sophophobic,' continued Mr P.

'What does that mean?'

'It's a fear of learning.'

'It's not a fear, dude, it's just hard work and you are too lazy.'

'This is true, Geoffrey, my man, but I do like silly long words.'

Mr P tried to end today's conversation with a funny one-liner. 'Just think, if you are afraid of time-travelling elephants wearing yellow hats then you are a chronophobic-pachydermophobium-xanthophobic-cocklaphoboid.'

They both laughed again.

'Especially if you're phallophobic,' chipped in Geoffrey. Geoffrey won the funny one-liners on that particular day.

Mystery at Hunters Lodge

Six weeks had passed since the visit to the time-hole, as it is now being called. And since then, Ivan and Frisby have become good friends, Geoffrey had started writing again, and Cleese had invented a new religion.

Mr P and Gertie had also been busy by acquiring a log cabin near to the banks of the great lakes in the valleys of restless mountains. They thought it was fantastic. The log cabin had history too. According to ancient human texts there had always been a structure on this exact site overlooking the Great Lakes, and over the years, the buildings had changed from stone structures to glass structures, and back to stone structures, but the footings and pathways had always remained the same. The current structure was erected about twenty-five years ago, when a retired postal worker built log cabin as a retreat away from the hustle and bustle of everyday life. And this was Hunters Lodge in all its glory.

In the winter the wind blows very cold, and snowstorms are a common feature. Access through the valleys can be tricky and very few ramblers dare to venture so far into the mountains. And it was on this night that Mr P and Gertie arrived at Hunters Lodge for a nice restful week away by the lakes.

Logey, the campervan, was rocking from side to side in the gale force winds as Mr P got out to make his way to the cabin. And he was instantly taken aback by the strong gales, and had to dig his heels into the ground for extra grip. It took some considerable effort to shut the van door, gather his bags from the side, and grab his hand-held lantern so he could see.

Now, hand held torches and flashlights were very commonplace, and very accessible, and very cheap. But Mr P much preferred to use an old lantern as a means of light. It was inconvenient and clumsy. It was prone to not working in the cold, and it needed gas to work — which is not very accessible, nor very cheap. However, it fitted in with his eccentric mannerisms, and he loved the fact that no one else would bother using it.

And so, in the swirling winds of the restless mountains, and with an old lantern held high, Mr P stumbled his way into Hunters Lodge to spend a relaxing weekend away with Gertie.

It took about two hours to light the log fire in the main living area and get some stew cooked, but once it was all done it was heavenly bliss. Gertie sat in front of the blazing log fire with her stew in one hand and a glass of wine in the other. She gazed into the flames and slowly began to unwind and relax into a thick cosy blanket. Mr P was sat to her side her looking through an old box of photographs that had been left in the cellar by the last owners of the lodge. Some of the photos were very old and some had begun to fade.

'You see how some of these photos are fading babe?' asked Mr P. 'That's because the ink that was used back then contained chromophores, which is a light absorbing chemical. I love old photos, it's a shame that we don't have 'em now.'

Gertie sipped on her wine and put her head into his shoulder. 'No, we have digital photos now that lasts forever,' she said sarcastically. 'But I do know what you mean. Not all progress is an improvement,' she added.

Mr P continued to pick his way through the old pictures. 'A lot of humans never smiled in old photographs,' he said in soft tone. 'Some think that it's because they had rotten teeth back then, but others say that the exposure time on the camera was so long that it was difficult to hold a smile for that long and the picture would come out blurry if they smiled. I think I would have smiled and risked a bit of blurriness.'

Gertie grinned and remained cosy in her blanket looking into the fire.

'Did you know that there was a mystery here at one time?' he continued. 'It was a bit like the Mary Celeste story really.'

Gertie slowly turned to face Mr P. 'What do you mean?' she asked.

'Well,' replied Mr P, 'the Mary Celeste was a boat that was found abandoned at sea in the late 1800s when humans lived on Earth. The boat should have had about ten sailors on board, but they all mysteriously disappeared. When it was found, their food was half eaten and warm, as if their fate was sudden and unexpected. To this day no one knows what happened to the crew. Their actions were so mysterious that it became folklore to the humans.'

Gertie sighed. 'What's that got to do with the lodge?'

'Well, a similar thing happened here in the late 1900s. Again, it was humans, but nevertheless it happened here. A group of humans were staying here for a weekend break when they all vanished without trace. When the owner came on Monday to clean, he found the table set for an evening meal, with the food half eaten. All their belongings were still in the drawers and wardrobes, and their phones and wallets still on the side where they would have been kept. It was just like they suddenly vanished. Very weird, eh?'

'Err yeah,' gasped Gertie. 'That's me not sleeping tonight.'

'Ha ha ha, don't be silly, babe,' laughed Mr P while continuing to flick through the old photos. 'There's always a rational explana...' Suddenly Mr P stopped talking, and definitely stopped laughing.

'What's up?' asked Gertie.

The grin had gone from his face and his eyes were wide open.

'It... It's Percival, babe.'

Mr P showed an old photograph to Gertie. 'Look, it's Percival, that human from the blue eternal lagoon at Pedn Vounder.'

Gertie looked closely at the photo. 'He looks almost exactly the same. Maybe a few years younger but that's all.'

'But this photograph is old, very old,' said Mr P now looking slightly worried. 'What are the odds on this? What are the odds that we met Percival and that we are here, in this log cabin, it must be million to one?'

He got up and walked over to the window that overlooked the lake. He couldn't see much as the snowstorm and the darkness of night hid all the features of the lakes but he continued to look out of the window. He turned to Gertie. 'Do you think it's fate? Are we meant to be here?'

Mr P was a big believer in fate. He had always had a sneaking impression that most things that had happened had been following a set path of which he had very little influence. Sure, you can change minor aspects of your life, but the big picture is set according to a master plan.

By this time Gertie was also looking through the old photos. She was paying very close attention to the fine details of the pictures, trying to make sense of the backgrounds and the ornaments within them.

'They are all human,' claimed Gertie, 'so these photos must be hundreds of years old, because every human left hundreds of years ago, and yet Percival looks only a few years younger.'

Mr P swiftly looked at Gertie. 'Time travel, babe,' he said. 'Simple, this is before he got left behind and had to hide inside Logan Rock.'

He walked over to the photos that were now scattered all over the floor. 'Look, there he is with his family, his wife and son, I bet that's who he went back to when we gave him the time machine, he is re-united with his family.'

They continued to frantically search through each photo looking for another clue. There were pictures of Percival and his son swimming in the lakes, a selfie of his wife and son on a paddle boat, a picture of Percival sitting on a fisherman's stool overlooking the lake.

'Wait... what's this?' screamed Gertie. 'It's a picture of Percival and Kice!'

'Nooo really,' answered Mr P, 'that is sooo weird. That means that Kice must have travelled back to that moment in time to be with Percival and his family, because we Dinglewits had not made it to Earth by that time. So why would he travel back in time to be with Percival? Why would he do that? Percival and his family would have been staggered to see a different species. What's the significance I wonder?'

Gertie's face lit up. 'Let's go investigate down the cellar, babe, there might be some more things to see. Oh, I wonder what we can find?' she urged Mr P.

Not that he needed any urging, he was all over it. He quickly put on his slippers, headed down the dark spiral stairs into the cellar, and pressed the light switch on the wall. The cellar lit up revealing about half a dozen more boxes all of which were sealed with brown tape, and one by one Mr P and Gertie opened them up and checked their contents. After about an hour all the boxes were opened but none of them contained anything inside of any importance.

Two boxes contained teddy bears; there were some old clothes in one box and some kitchen stuff in another. They looked at each other disappointedly.

'Well, there's nothing here,' claimed Gertie, 'just general household stuff that they stored here for some reason.'

'Yeah, but it's kinda strange that they left all this stuff here like this. Teddy bears! You don't just discard teddy bears, and kitchen stuff, and clothes. No, these things were stored here to be collected and un-boxed later I reckon,' answered Mr P.

They scoured the cellar for another minute before deciding to call it a night and head back upstairs. However, just as Gertie was about to turn out the light, she saw something glistening in a dark corner. 'What's that?' she asked, and began walking towards the object. As Gertie got closer, she could see it was an old bowl made from rock that was sat on top of an old book.

'Babe, I think it's an old rock bowl and a diary,' said Gertie in a confused tone.

'Really?' added Mr P, as he walked over to take hold of the book. He picked it up, shook off some of the dust, and cleared the rest of the dust with his hand. It looked old and written on the front was:

The personal diary of George Saxe-Coburg and Gotha

'Oh, my diggety dog, Gertie, look at this. It's the diary of King George. It's the missing King George V diary. Wow. This is a priceless artefact, babe.'

Gertie looked staggered. 'What is this though?' she asked holding up the rock bowl. 'It looks old.'

Mr P agreed. 'Yeah, it does, it's probably an ancient human relic of some sort.'

He moved the bowl around a few times in his hand before handing it over to Gertie. 'The rock probably isn't worth anything though, it looks like agate, but if you look on one side you can see that it was used as a drinking bowl. It's still pretty neat though.'

'Oh cool,' came a rather unusual response from Gertie. 'I'm keeping it, it's pretty. I'll put it on top of the fireplace.'

Mr P kept hold of the book and gave the bowl to Gertie.

It was quite chilly in the cellar and with nothing else to see they headed back upstairs to the warmth of the lodge. They sat down in silence, put their arms around each other and began to read the diary entitled

"The personal diary of George Saxe-Coburg and Gotha" in front of the burning fire.

They read all night and were amazed at the journey that this ancient human monarch enjoyed. There was page after page of human history, written first hand by one of the most powerful people to have ever lived. There were tales of wars and conquests, and of new knowledge and inventions, the excitement of new eras and epochs being born, and the formation of new ideas and societies.

As they read through each chapter and each adventure it was clear that the king was optimistic about the future, and how the world will work itself out. He wrote about the future, like a little boy would write tales in a schoolbook, as he sought to make sense of what he was seeing in a rationality that was as innocent as the 20th century. For them, however, it was all in the past, all the things that were written by this exuberant ruler they had read before, in history books and in cryptic books. For although this was all new for King George, to Mr P and Gertie it was ancient history, and had been played out. All except for one chapter, this was the chapter with the heading "The World of 3560". These pages had been crudely ripped out of the diary leaving a ragged edge down the spine of the book.

'Why had this chapter been removed?' thought Mr P to himself. What happened in the year 3560 that was so special that it needed to be removed? This would have been the most interesting chapter for Mr P and

Gertie because it would have given them an insight into the future that they were yet to witness. Was the future so bizarre that even this time travelling sovereign felt the need to remove it from his diary? Or had someone else removed it?

This puzzled them, especially due to what had been left in the diary such as the meeting with Aristarchus of Samos to discuss the shape of the Earth; a view of the New World Order that materialised in 2033, a meeting with Isaac Newton in 1665 to warn him of the Great Plague and to advise him to move to his childhood home in Woolsthorpe-by-Colsterworth in order to preserve his unique intellect, and even a trip back to ancient Egypt to witness the building of the step pyramid of Djoser, but still the chapter on the year 3560 had been removed.

'Why do you think this has been removed, babe?' asked Gertie. 'I don't like things like this, it makes me scared of what might happen.'

'It is curious,' he answered, 'that somebody, somewhere wanted it removed, I wonder why?'

There was a silence that was deafening, and was only broken by Gertie getting up to pour another drink. They continued to look through the diary amazed at the experiences that King George had had. Amazing stories and adventures and a life lived to the full, however, beneath the elegant words and crudely drawn pictures they couldn't escape from the lost chapter of the year 3560.

'Well, I'm going to bed,' she said.

And with that she walked into the bedroom, leaving Mr P contemplating the diary; in front of a blazing fire, in a lodge in the middle of a snowstorm, and in the wilderness of the valleys overlooked by the restless mountains.

Morning shower

As morning dawned Gertie had woken up earlier than normal. Mr P was still laid on the floor wrapped up in the warm blanket from the night before, but as he began to show signs of life, he could tell that Gertie had been looking through a box of old books that she had brought upstairs from the cellar. The box was now half empty and to one side were two piles of old books. Some of the book covers were tattered and torn while others looked almost new.

The books on top of each pile were left open as if deliberately placed there in order to be read. The agate rock bowl was placed on the mantlepiece; full of potpourri, overlooking an old rug that itself was in front of the fireplace. Outside the window the snowstorm was still raging but the warmth from the fire inside the lodge allowed for a pleasant and comfortable start to the day. Gertie was in the kitchen wearing thick winter socks and shorts, and making a large saucepan of chilli that gave the lodge a pleasant smell that added to its warmth. He could not get his head around the fact that Dinglewits and humans had met, and no one had documented it, or probably not even known about the meeting.

There is not a single known case of the two species ever being in the same vicinity, and yet, here is proof that it happened. Why? Mr P kept asking himself. He couldn't believe that it was just for vanity, or for a sense of gratuitous curiosity. No, Mr P was convinced that the meeting was a part of something big, something special. And he wanted to know what. He found it hard to believe that the rulers and leaders, who pretty much owned the universe and its wealth and use their money entirely for their own pleasure, hadn't have found this diary by now. So how come it was just abandoned here in a wooden old lodge under a worthless agate rock bowl? It made no sense to him. Were Ivan's employers these very same rich people? Or were they a resistance group with a mysterious and secret benefactor that wanted to find the enigmas of the universe and the origins of the existence of life and prevent it from being distorted by the establishment?

Gertie stopped mixing the chilli and walked into the room from the kitchen. She walked slowly but purposely and gently bent down to take the diary from the hands of Mr P. She held it in front of her for a while casually flicking through a few pages then handed it back.

'Have you considered that this diary was hidden here for a purpose?' she asked.

This confused Mr P. He looked at the old book to try and give him the answers. 'Just consider this,' she said, 'clearly Percival had the ability to time travel at some point because he had lost his loved ones to time, he certainly had Oocohol, and we know that Kice had a time machine because he sold it to you, and that they had the ability to travel to 2033 because they had the coin. And we now know that the two of them have met, which therefore means that the Oocohol and the time machine were available to them at some point. Now the question is, when was this photograph taken? I would say that it was taken before the events that saw Kice move to Marrakesh, and Percival hide out in a cave at Logan Rock. So the question is, why? Why did they go their separate ways? And why did they leave a precious diary here under an ancient rock bowl?'

'Well,' replied Mr P, 'they could only go to 2033 if they were in the time wormhole machine and if they had the coin, otherwise they would have to time travel in just the traditional way. Which therefore means that the coin was of very little use to them except for its ability to make them invisible from modern technology of CCTV and robots and satellites and the like. Which is probably why they were willing to give it up as thank you presents. The bigger question is how did they get hold of it in the first place, because I'm assuming that they would have been very valuable to someone when they were made. But then that doesn't answer the question of why did they meet?'

Gertie frowned and put each of her index fingers onto each reciprocal eye, and gave them a gentle rub.

'Let's check the diary again to see if any clues are in it,' she stated.

Mr P leaned over and picked up the diary from down the side of the sofa where it had fallen during the night. They both sat next to each other on the floor in front of the sofa and began flicking through the pages. They casually flicked through the pages glancing at sub-headings for clues of what might be in the text before quickly moving on if it wasn't deemed interesting, until they got to a drawing. As with the other drawings it was more like a doodle and was in the bottom right of the page entitled "our visit to Saint Martin du Champs". On first glance the drawing did not look very interesting, as did the visit to an ancient villa, but they recognised the object in the drawing, it was the rock bowl they had found in the cellar.

Underneath the drawing were the words "The Holy Grail".

Mr P and Gertie looked up to the mantelpiece at the agate rock bowl, now full of potpourri, and stared, and stared, and stared.

'Oh my God,' screamed Gertie, 'we have filled the holy grail with fucking potpourri!'

She jumped up from the floor, ran over to the mantelpiece and picked up the grail with both hands. Then just as quick she put it back down again. 'What are we gonna do?' she asked.

'Oh jeez,' replied Mr P, 'we should just leave it here for now, Gertie, we don't want this getting out or there will be consequences for us, and not good ones I would imagine.'

'How do you mean?' Gertie asked.

'Err, well, err, well it's quite simple really, Gertie. That Jesus of Nazareth human chap is famous yeah. And this is the Holy Grail, probably the most prized artefact in existence. There are some that are fascinated by this stuff and would do anything to have it. I don't see any good in bringing this whole grail thingy to light. In fact, the fact that this George character stole the grail is probably the reason why it was never found. No, I say we leave it here and keep shush.'

'But it was found,' Gertie remarked. 'It was found and was stolen by King George, and then obviously somebody else stole it, and now we have it. We have the most important object in the history of the universe, and someone somewhere knows that it is here.'

Mr P picked up the bowl. 'Wow, the Holy Grail, babe. We need a plan!'

'I need a drink,' Gertie replied, 'and don't even think about selling it!' she shouted. Mr P frowned and sat back down on the sofa. 'What shall we do with it then?' he asked.

Gertie already knew the answer. 'We are going to return it. I don't know how, but we are going to give it back. This is way too big for us, so ring your friends and talk to whomever, but it goes back. Oh, my goodness. I'm going for a shower, you coming?'

Then Gertie stripped naked in front of Mr P and walked off.

Mr P wasn't really interested in religion to be fair, and phoning people was the last thing on his mind at that moment in time, so he got up from the sofa and put the grail back on the mantelpiece and joined Gertie in the shower.

They had a good morning.

Percival

Sir Percival was one of King Arthur's most trusted knights and was awarded the honour of guarding the Holy Grail for all eternity, an honour for which Percival was humbled and vowed never to betray. Now, Arthurian legend tells us that the Holy Grail was taken from the table of the last supper by Joseph of Arimathea, where it eventually ended up in Glastonbury cathedral where it was to be guarded by the Knights Templar. Following the destruction of the cathedral by King Henry VIII, the location of the grail became a mystery, with some scholars theorising that it was kept at Rosslyn Chapel, while others claimed that it was transported to Rome. However, the truth is this.

Joseph of Arimathea did indeed take the grail from the table of the last supper, where, following the crucifixion of Christ they fled the Romans and entered into Europe. While on the long and dangerous journey, they stopped and rested at various holy places and buildings such as, the castle of Corbenic, the convent of Christ castle in Tomar, and also the chateau of Saint Martin du Champs, where they met with Sir Percival while on his grail quest. This is where the grail was transferred from Joseph's care and into Percival's, with the knowledge that it would be safe in his hands, and knowing that the greatest artefact in human history would be preserved forever.

Percival then headed to the outermost known region of the Earth, called Britannia, where he and his true love, Angharad, hid in a remote cave and drank from the sacred water of the lagoon in order to preserve their lives for all eternity.

There was only one problem with this plan. Angharad got bored. She wanted kids. She wanted to move to a more desirable area and have evening lunches with her friends. Thus, family problems arose. And as time went by, Angharad would leave the seclusion of the cave to have a social life, and eventually, she formed a friendship group of which Percival was excluded.

Percival of course was still completely devoted to his task of guarding the Holy Grail and the loss of his love would not change this. Angharad would never love another, but for her, the thought of an eternity in a cave was not as appealing as she had first assumed, and so in 2053, just before the mass exodus of humans from planet Earth, she left Pedn Vounder and re-joined society. Percival thought he would never see her again.

That is not until two mysterious, and funny looking aliens from the planet Luyten b walked into his cave, and offered him a second chance.

Following their discussion, and the parting of ways, Percival decided that he had finished in his task, and as the humans no longer inhabit the Earth, he should now go and find his Angharad. Percival did not take this decision lightly of course, and as he sat on his seat made from rock overlooking the lagoon of eternal life he made a decision, and that was to entrust the Holy Grail into the care of the two mysterious aliens — Mr P and Gertie. To Percival, the fact that these two adventurers were brave enough to enter the cave, and were benevolent enough to give him a time machine, meant that it must be a sign from God. He took this to be a sign that it is they, who must now be the rightful guardians of the cup of Christ.

In the morning Percival gathered a few clothes together and put them in a scruffy old leather carry bag, grabbed his trusty old sword that he had had for over a thousand years, and wrapped the Holy Grail in a blanket. He still had the Liberty Coin that was given to him by Mr P and Gertie, although this now felt a bit surplus to requirements. Nevertheless he put it in his pocket and bent over to have one final slurp from the lagoon, before exiting the cave forever. He made his way up the rock face, that he hadn't seen for hundreds of years, and found the silver Norma Red that had been left for him. He carefully placed the grail on the passenger seat and put the bag on the floor of the passenger footwell. He knew that this was the end of an era, and that he would never see the beautiful sunset over the Cornish beach ever again. He sat and pondered for a few seconds. His life from now on would be different, and the only way that Angharad would believe him, is if he could visibly show her he had changed.

'I know,' he thought to himself, 'they can have my sword as a token of my appreciation. Oh, and the coin as well, after all they have given me a second chance at life.

But always being the dramatist, he decided to replace the Norma Red with the biggest rock he could muster. Now having drunk from the lagoon of eternal life for so many years had given Percival immense strength. And with that strength he picked up a huge rock from the cliff's edge and carried it back to the car.

'Ahh yes,' he proudly thought to himself, 'this will impress them.' He then took a pen and paper and wrote:

My good friends,

This coin is yours I believe.

It has more value than you could ever know, and it belongs with you. It is very rare, and it has abilities yet to be discovered.

Be careful of its power.

Good luck with your travels.

Percival

He placed the note underneath the Liberty Coin, leant his sword by its side, and set the time machine to 2053, and then he was gone, gone to try and find his true love.

Debbie

Within a flash he arrived at 2053. He had noted the way
that Angharad was dressed when she left and tried to
wear attire that he felt was similar, but apparently
according to a rather rude young boy he 'looked like
something from the 2040s dude.' Percival paid it no
attention; his mind was set on finding his Angharad.

The new world was a very strange place. Everywhere
he looked, people were rushing around, as if time were
against them, and as if they were in competition with
each other. Percival didn't much care for this way of life
but until he found Angharad he was stuck here, and
maybe he was stuck here for life as he had used up the
last of the Oocohol. He decided that action was required
and so he did the only thing that he could to find
Angharad; he went onto social media to find her. He
typed in Angharad but the only face that appeared was
of a woman call Debbie Angharad. He looked closely,
then even closer, was this his true love hiding behind
pouting lips and a very clever filter? 'I think it is,' he
said out loud. 'It's her! It's her!' and began dancing a
very dodgy dad dance in the middle of the street.

The phone call was short and sweet, and within ten
minutes they were back in each other's arms. For

Angharad, she had not seen Percival in weeks and she was so happy that he had chosen to find her and give up his old way of life. For Percival, he had not seen her in hundreds of years and felt desperate without her. And as they stood there, cuddled together in the middle of the street time had no meaning.

'I have to go to work,' whispered Angharad with tears in her eyes and rubbing her nose to get rid of the overflow. 'I start my new job today, come with me?'

'Of course,' replied Percival. 'What is it you do for work?'

'I work for the W.H.O. I'm a secretary and I have to write the minutes to a conference call on climate change today. It's my first day. I work from home so it's no bother for you to be there.'

'OK, but why are you now called Debbie?' asked Percival.

'I needed to fit in to get a job, and Debbie is the trendy name at the moment, so I just used that,' she replied.

'Oh,' replied Percival, half expecting some deep and meaningful reason for the name change.

And we already know the consequences of Debbie writing the minutes at the climate change meeting!

They spent the night together, and had such a good night, that they both slept in in the morning.

King George

It wasn't long after they had woken before Percival and Angharad realised what had happened and that they were now the only humans left on the planet.

'Well, I don't know what's happened here, Angharad, but someone has made a massive mistake,' stated Percival.

'Yeah weird,' replied Angharad 'but this planet was always full of numpties. But why has everyone left? Is there something we should know?'

They were both blissfully unaware of the actual reason why the entire population of the planet upped sticks and left, but they were glad for the peace and quiet. They had just taken residence in an old hunting lodge where they could collect their thoughts and spend some time together.

Angharad had had a torrid couple of nights sleep and was now looking forward to getting her head down in silence. Percival was in deep thought. He still had the Holy Grail in his possession and was hoping to palm it off onto Mr P and Gertie, but of course they weren't here yet as the Dinglewits were still making their way through the coldness of intergalactic space. That said the decision had been made and his mind was set, he was giving up on the Holy Grail to live a normal life, and so he pondered his next move.

Angharad was asleep on the sofa and Percival had just made a cup of tea. He was settling down to read a good book when he saw a stranger suddenly appear in the garden. As the stranger walked slowly towards him, he recognised his face, he had met him before, but a long, long, time ago.

'Angharad, Angharad, wake up,' he whispered in her ear while also shaking her by the shoulders. 'There is someone in the garden.'

Angharad slowly opened her eyes and moved her head slowly from side to side. 'Who is it?' she asked.

'I don't know but I think I recognise him.'

'Here, let me take a look, oh yeah it's Galahad,' stated Angharad. 'How come he is here, surely he must be dead by now!'

'Yeah, he should be,' answered Percival. He walked towards the back door and opened it up to let his old friend in.

'Sir Galahad, my old friend, how the devil are you?' shouted Percival. 'It's great to see you again.'

Galahad stopped and bent down on one knee to honour the sight of the guardian of the Holy Grail. 'Sir Percival,' replied Galahad. There was a moment of mutual respect between the two great noblemen of the round table. They were never the greatest of friends having only seen each other a few times, and on each occasion, in the company of King Arthur while in the Kingdom of Camelot.

'Come in come in,' said Percival while gesturing Galahad to into his house, 'you must be thirsty but it's great timing as I've just made a pot of tea, take a seat.'

Sir Galahad looked slightly older than when they last met, but of course that was thousands of years ago so it is to be expected. He had put a bit of weight on, his beard was not as long, and he walked in a more crouched position. He had aged — something that Percival had not.

'Percival, I have something I need to tell you,' Galahad stated, 'and it's important that you pay close attention.'

This got the attention of both Percival and Angharad, and they both joined Sir Galahad on the sofa.

'What is on your mind, Sir?' asked Percival.

Galahad began. 'Sir Percival, Lady Angharad, first of all let me introduce myself to you properly. My name is George Frederick Ernest Albert and I am formally known as King George V of England.'

This took Percival and Angharad by surprise, they both sat upright on the sofa clutching each other's hands. George continued, 'I adopted the name of Galahad during my visits with King Arthur, but I'm really George Saxe-Coburg the King of the English.'

'Nooo,' answered Percival, 'how did you manage all that?'

'I was able to travel through time with seven coins that I had made. Each coin takes you to a different time frame through the portals that are scattered around the country.'

'Yes, we had one of the coins,' answered Percival.

'Well, they are valuable and can be used for good in the right hands but used for ill in the wrong ones. Do you still have it?' asked George.

'No, I gave it to someone worthy,' replied Percival.

'Good, I still have two coins here; I know who have the other four so they are all accounted for. It is important that we guard these coins as they are the key to the Earth and all its secrets,' George stated.

Percival grabbed George's hand. 'It's OK, old friend, together we will make sure that they are safe.'

George looked up at Percival with a look that Percival had seen many times. It was the look that somebody gives you when they know that they will never see you again.

'I won't be able to I'm afraid,' said George. 'I'm dying and I don't have long left. I need you to ensure their safe keeping.'

'Of course I will, you can count on me,' Percival answered.

George continued. 'Scattered around the island are time portals that if you enter with the coins will transport you to an exact moment in time. These are historic sites such as Stonehenge, Glastonbury Tor, Temple church and so on, there are lots of them — you just have to enter them with a coin. I have been using them for years and have seen a great many things. But now my time is up and I can no longer experience the greatness of time that God has gifted me. Do you still have the Holy Grail?'

'Yes.'

'Can I hold it one last time?'

'Of course, it's over there.' Percival pointed to the table where the grail was sitting.

George got up and walked over to hold the Earth's most precious relic for one last time.

'It's beautiful,' he said with a tear in his eye, 'but it has one last surprise,' and with that he turned the cup upside down and inserted a coin into a perfectly carved out hollow.

George continued, 'When Joseph of Arimathea left Jerusalem he carved a slot in the grail so he could hide a gold coin inside just in case he got stopped by the Romans. He presumed that they wouldn't be interested in a rock cup and if they stole his other items, he would still have a gold coin. The size of the gold coin was used as exact dimensions for my penny. I have placed the seventh coin inside and I want you to have the sixgh.'

With that George handed a coin over to Percival. 'Thank you, old friend, I will keep it safe.'

Percival said. George took one last look at the Holy Grail and placed it back onto the table.

Percival continued. 'How will you get back to your time if you don't have a coin?'

'Oh, it's not a problem, I have a lift with this chap,' George answered, as he pointed to a very strange creature now standing at the door. 'He is an alien from the future.'

And with that the strange creature walked forward into the house. 'Helloooo,' he said, 'my name is Kice, it's a pleasure to meet you.'

Percival and Angharad stood frozen to the spot; Percival had seen his kind before. He was the same species as Mr P and Gertie and he must have travelled here from the future.

'How do you do?' remarked Percival offering his hand to Kice.

'I am fine, thank you,' came the reply. 'You don't seem surprised by my existence if I may be bold to say.'

'That is because I have seen your species before. I was visited by two of your kind while I was in my cave inside Logan Rock,' Percival answered 'you sent them to me.'

Now it was Kice's turn to be surprised, but it was a strange kind of day, and so with that they all sat down and had a cup of tea. They talked for hours telling each other of their stories and explaining the things that had happened like it happened only yesterday, and over the next few hours they had covered the entire history of life on Earth. In fact by the end of the night Percival and Kice were getting on like good friends. They spoke of wars and of inventions, and of great people and of evil people — all the things that make up the history of a species. They even spoke about the year 3560, and it was agreed by all that the pages in the diary concerning the events of that year should be removed. So they tore out the pages and put them on the fire, never to be seen by bipedal eyes again.

However, as the night came to a close George stood up. 'I'm afraid we need to go,' he said, 'shall we do photos to mark the occasion?'

'That is a splendid idea,' chipped in Percival, and they took it in turns posing for the camera. After a few, rather choice, photos Percival and George shook hands and walked out of the house together with their arms around each other.

Angharad followed closely behind with Kice at the back, but as he walked out, he saw a coin on the table near to the grail. The grail was too big to steal but the coin, well, the coin could easily go into his pocket and not be detected. And that is exactly what happened. And so the penny that Mr P and Gertie was to be given by Kice, that had been stolen by Kice from Percival, that had been given to Percival by King George V (nee Sir Galahad) began its never-ending journey — lost in the loop of time.

Percival spent an uneasy night suspecting that Kice had taken a coin, but rather than getting upset took a more pragmatic approach. After all he did not want the coin in the first place, he didn't even want the Holy Grail. So why not. Let Kice have the coin. In fact, he was going to go one further. He picked up the Holy

Grail, went down into the cellar and placed it in a dark corner.

'There,' he said. 'I shall leave the grail to the fate of time.' Percival then went back upstairs and never thought of it again.

The Knights Templar and the Holy Grail

Percival had been given the challenge of looking after the grail for the last millennia and now the baton had been passed on to Mr P and Gertie — for now at least. In the meantime, there was still the meaning of life to be understood, and there were some questions that still remained unanswered. In Mr P's notebook he had made good progress so far in detailing the things that are important, but there still seemed an element of unfinished business. Sure he had more tools at his disposal now than when he started out on this adventure such as the Liberty Coin, knowledge of time travel and the ability to travel back to various points in time due to his new acquaintances, the supposed Holy Grail, and a few connections with very clever scientists. Oh, and not forgetting money, Mr P was renting the Liberty Coin to Ivan's employers, and was now getting a good monthly wage as a result of the deal, which allowed him time to pursue other activities. However, there was still something missing. It felt like there was an empty hole that required filling. Mr P had been toying with the word "self-actualisation" which had been something he had read on one of his more spiritual days, and he knew that he hadn't quite achieved it yet.

Is anyone truly self-actualised? he thought as he sat down on the porch of Hunters Lodge with a glass of iced punch in one hand and his notebook in the other. Surely it is natural Dinglewit behaviour to strive for more and to constantly wish for better. Isn't that why we work so hard so we can have the nicer things in life?

He had written many aspects of his journey to find the meaning of life so far, but on the front page were his main themes. They read:

Be inquisitive Be adventurous. Be magical.
Be nice.
And be open-minded, but still there seemed something was missing, however, first there was the mission of returning something to its rightful place.

On its journey into Britannia from the Garden of Gethsemane, the grail was once stored in the chateau of Saint Martin du Champs, and as Mr P and Gertie couldn't be absolutely sure of specific times or dates this seemed as good a place as any to return it. In the history books they had read about the Fisher King as this mythical figure with the most important job in the universe, and now that was them, they were a part of history — if anyone ever found out that is. Mr P revelled in this new title. He had a badge custom-made reading "Mr P — the Fisher King", which he wore constantly, and he had a bumper sticker attached to Logey the campervan stating the same. Gertie refused to indulge in this odious frivolity and constantly nagged Mr P to take his badge off every time they were likely to be seen by Dinglewits they knew. Mr P figured that this is probably the only time in his life that he could wear such a tag, and that it is actually true, so he was going to make the most of it.

Not knowing where to start they contacted Ivan and asked him for his help to get them back to biblical times, naturally he was inquisitive, but they felt that some discretion would be best advised. He agreed to help but offered a stark warning, these were the times of the Knights Templar and they will defend what they believe to the death. The chateau of Saint Martin du Champs was a Templar building and they will not take an intrusion lightly, this was a dangerous mission and one, in the eyes of Gertie, they didn't need to make, but sat on the porch of Hunters Lodge with a glass of iced punch and his notebook Mr P removed a green crayon from his pocket and wrote:

The meaning of life — 6) Live a little dangerously

'Sometimes you need to live a little dangerously to know you are still alive,' Mr P told Gertie. 'This is a once in a lifetime adventure and the entire history of the world may depend on our actions.'

'Well,' replied Gertie, 'no pressure there then, eh? What's your plan?'

'Err I ain't really got one,' stated Mr P. 'I'm sort of hoping to drop the Holy Grail off and leave without being slaughtered.'

'Sounds like a good plan to me,' said Gertie sarcastically. 'Do you want me to come?'

'Of course I do, babe, if the adventure doesn't include you, then it isn't worth doing. Even if the adventure is getting brutally slaughtered,' came the soppy reply.

Gertie walked over and put her arms around Mr P as if to acknowledge the romantic sentiment, even if it was one that might get her killed.

Ivan was worried about the chances of Mr P and Gertie escaping should anything untoward happen, and was even more concerned if the entire LPMD team went. Of course they were practically invisible to humans due to them being on a different time dimension, but there are a lot of time tourists that travel to that moment in history, and so danger could easily be had. That said Cleese was very keen to tag along, being as he was, a wizard. Geoffrey was not quite so keen.

The Knights Templar was an ancient human cult that swore an oath to defend all of Christendom and its relics from destruction, one of which was the Holy Grail. They had failed drastically attempting to guard the Arc of the Covenant, and now the Holy Grail had mysteriously vanished. Hugues de Payens was apoplectic with rage and vowed to find it on pains of death. He had travelled throughout Europe looking to find clues as to how it had suddenly vanished but could not fathom it out. He dispatched Hugh, the Count of Champagne, back to Jerusalem to trace their steps, while Hugues himself was visiting all the Templar safe havens. It was in this time of upheaval that Mr P, Gertie, Cleese, had decided to travel back in time too. Geoffrey was invited but he wimped out and waited outside.

They felt like there was no time like the present , and as Ivan had managed to borrow the appropriate coin, they walked over to the church at St. Sennen and entered via the secret door to the side. They were to enter the time cycle at the 12th century, which seemed about right to them, Ivan was also pretty confident that this was the most appropriate time to enter history. They knew from the history books that Hugues de Payens entered England near here, so maybe they would get lucky. And so as three of the four members of the LPMD entered the history books, Geoffrey and Ivan waited outside with instructions should they not return in the next few seconds.

The church at St. Sennen is a magical place, with candles lit all day round and a feeling that the world's history has been through their doors. It is in the middle of nowhere, and most of the year there is a mist surrounding it due to its location and the scarcity of other buildings. Mr P entered the church first followed closely by Gertie and Cleese. Cleese had brought along a homemade sword that had taken him two years to bend and bash until the metal was of the required concentration. He was immensely proud of his sword, and it was testament to the importance of this cause that he had decided to bring it along.

They stood side-by-side staring at the alter for a few seconds before Gertie broke the silence. 'Come on then,' she said, 'we ain't got all day.'

And with those poignant words of momentous importance, they walked toward destiny.

In a flash they could tell that the air had changed. The fresh air within the church had turned to a musky smell of cattle and excrement. Mr P sniffed a few times before looking at Gertie, she looked back and put her fingers over her nose and turned to Cleese. Cleese was not fazed by the smell but in fact he was looking transfixed and with a tear in his eyes.

'You OK?' asked Gertie.

Cleese didn't reply, he remained looking forward and within a few seconds he dropped onto one knee and placed his sword on the alter beside him. 'Dude?' asked Mr P 'you still with us?'

'I'm home,' came the reply. Mr P and Gertie both laughed.

'What are you on about mate?' asked Mr P. 'C'mon, let's go!'

Cleese didn't reply, instead he decided to lay prone on the floor with his arms in front of him. Mr P and Gertie took one quick glimpse at each other and turned and walked off. 'We ain't got time for that weirdo,' she said.

Gertie was holding the Holy Grail.

As they walked out of the main door, they could see a gathering of humans outside.

They looked important as they were wearing extravagant materials but in very dark colours.

'Look?' said Gertie, 'they are all wearing hats.'

'I do like a good hat,' replied Mr P while using both hands to correct the position of his own.

'Are we invisible to them, babe?' asked Gertie.

'I dunno, but best not to risk it,' answered Mr P 'Let's go this way,' he said taking Gertie by the hand and leading her to the side and around some gravestones. They crouched down and watched the proceedings from behind their secluded hiding place. The group of men continued to talk for a few minutes before turning and heading out of the church grounds. All except one, the vicar, he turned and headed back into the church. Mr P and Gertie were worried about Cleese, being as he was, laid face down on the stone floor.

'What shall we do?' asked Gertie.

'Nothing we can do.'

'Let's go and have a look.' Gertie could be quite adventurous when she wanted to be. And so, with great caution, they both slowly moved back into the church of St. Sennen.

As they entered the church there was seating to the left and to the right — the alter is to the right. Mr P and Gertie thought it best to stay well away from any human contact and decided to turn left and sit on the pews at the back of the church. They could see the vicar walking towards the alter, and they could see that Cleese had now stood up and was looking directly at the vicar. They couldn't be sure what the vicar was seeing. They were supposed to be on a different time dimension, but according to Ivan, it is possible that humans could see them as a kind of mirage, or a ghostly type figure, from the actions of the vicar Mr P and Gertie were sure that he could see something. Cleese was wearing a long coat with the hood up and had his sword in his right hand facing down towards the floor. If they didn't know better even, they could have been fooled into thinking that Cleese was a ghost or a divine spirit.

The vicar dropped to his knees, bowed, and began to pray. This was bad news, as now they knew that they can be seen and could be in real danger if they weren't careful. Gertie grabbed the Holy Grail and they quickly left the church while the vicar was otherwise preoccupied. They ran down the path leading up to the main entrance and headed towards a wooded area. By the time they got there they were both out of breath. They ventured into the woods being extra careful not to disturb too many branches on the way until they arrived at a lake. And there they sat for around five minutes thinking about what to do next. They hadn't anticipated being visible to the humans and thought that the plan of dropping the Holy Grail off and returning would be easy. Now they had to rethink.

'Well,' chirped in Gertie, 'now what?'

Mr P didn't answer straight away; he was looking around at the lake. It was beautiful. He had seen nice lakes before but this one seemed to have a glow about it. The lake was surrounded by low-lying rocks and as the sun began to fade the elements within the rocks glistened. Mr P stood and walked to the lake's side and stood staring out into it for a few seconds as if prisoned by its beauty.

He turned to Gertie and pointed at the Holy Grail. 'Babe, the grail, it's shining,' he said.

Gertie looked down to where she had placed the grail. 'Wow,' she answered, 'it is shining, it's like a soft glow.'

'How can that be?' asked Mr P. 'It wasn't glowing earlier.' He was right while they were in the church of St. Sennen the grail was just the usual rock colour as it had been all the while, but now that they are near the lake it began to glow. It wasn't a full-blown glow however and both Mr P and Gertie knew instinctively that this was a sign.

'It seems to be attracted to the lake, babe, perhaps being near it is making it glow,' Mr P cautiously said.

'Yeah, or perhaps it has started to glow because it is near to where it should be, if it hadn't been taken from its own timeline,' Gertie answered.

'That's brilliant, babe, perhaps we should keep moving until we found the exact place,' added Mr P.

Gertie agreed and so they began walking slowly around the lake looking for a change to the glow of the grail. They kept walking for some time until they noticed that it had gone pitch black. Only the light from the moon could be seen.

'Oh, my goodness,' said Gertie while looking up at the sky. 'Look at that beautiful sky, you can see all the stars perfectly.'

'That's because there are no artificial lights to drown out the beauty,' answered Mr P. 'Amazing ain't it?'

They both stood there transfixed to the stars until they heard the rustling of a few trees about 20 metres away. It was the vicar; he was walking down to the lake. He too was mesmerized, presumably because he had mistaken Cleese for sort of spiritual vision. He walked into a shallow part of the lake and got on both knees and began praying. Mr P and Gertie instinctively starting walking towards him and as they did the grail began to glow ever brighter.

'Be careful, Gertie,' said Mr P and they approached the vicar.

'It's OK, babe, this does not feel dangerous in any way,' she replied.

As they got to the lake's edge, Mr P stopped but Gertie kept walking. She walked into the lake and in the direction of the vicar, and every step she took the grail glowed brighter and brighter. As she approached the vicar, she could see a singular rock protruding from the lake. It had a flat part on top and it looked too perfect for it to simply be a coincidence. Gertie took a look at the rock and slowly walked over to it. As she did the vicar noticed her and followed her movements with his head.

As she approached the rock the grail began to glow ever brighter so she kept going.

The vicar did not say a word and as Gertie got to the rock the grail erupted into a blaze of light. She placed it on the rock and slowly turned around and walked back towards Mr P. Once Gertie was a safe distance away the vicar got up from his knees and headed for the Holy Grail.

As he picked it up, he yelled. 'I, Lancelot, take possession of the cup of Christ and I shall guard it for all eternity.'

Gertie got back to the edge of the lake where Mr P was waiting. 'Well,' she said, 'that's that then, shall we go home?'

'Aye,' he replied. 'Let's get Cleese and get out of here.' And they started making their way back up to the church.

As they began to walk in brisk but controlled way back to their own time they heard a rumbling in the distance. It was vaguely like the sound of a pride of lions running towards them like a herd of buffalos.

'What's that noise?' asked Gertie as they both stopped and looked around in different directions.

'I don't know, babe,' Mr P replied, 'but I don't like the sound of it, it sounds really close. We should hide.'

Gertie thought this was a brilliant idea and she pointed to an abandoned barn just off the path that led to the church. The brisk walk was now a flat out run and they knew that they were now in danger. The barn door was damaged and there was no lock to stop intruders from getting in. They quickly opened the door by lifting it slightly to prevent it from dragging on the path and they both went inside. It was dark and the air inside was very musky and damp. Mr P knelt down by the door and peeped through one of the many damaged slits so he had a good view of the church. The pathway and entrance up to the church seemed very different in the low light than it did in the daytime. There was a luminescence around the church and the rays of the moonlight brushed off the ancient roofing giving a green tinge to the whole area. As they walked up to the main entrance, they could see Cleese standing in the doorway. He had a glow around him also and he looked remarkably human from the small parts of his face that could be seen. It became suddenly apparent to Mr P that Cleese fitted in here, his long beard, his lanky frame, his slow-moving demeanour, and his personality. This is where Cleese was meant to be and had he been born in this era he would have fitted in perfectly.

The rumbling came louder and louder and the earth vibrated between under their feet. Gertie had taken to hiding in some straw at the back of the barn but Mr P had no such thoughts. This was an adventure of a lifetime and he did not want to miss a thing. The rumblings grew louder and louder and the vibrations grew stronger and stronger. Mr P could see Cleese still standing by the entrance to the church. He was not moving and he did not seem at all worried by the advancing herd of animals — if that is what they were. As the rumblings grew loud enough to be almost on top of them the pace of their running seemed to slow as if they were slowing down to walking pace. Mr P continued to stare at the church entrance through the slits in the barn door and he did not take his eyes off Cleese who now appeared calmer than ever.

'Halt!' shouted Cleese as he extended both arms out totally blocking the entrance to the church. And with that the herd began to slow down to a walking pace. Mr P turned his head to the left and saw creatures that he could have never in his life imagined — it was the body of a lion but with wings and a head of an eagle, and there were loads of them.

'Gertie!' whispered Mr P, to the now hiding Gertie. 'Come and see this.' Gertie appeared from under the straw and with the appearance of a scarecrow joined Mr P at the barn door. 'Have you ever seen anything like those before?' Mr P asked Gertie.

'Yes,' came the remarkable reply, 'they are Griffins, wow they really did exist.'

'Gr… Griffins… are they dangerous?' Mr P responded.

'Oh god yes, we best stay here,' Gertie answered, 'we don't wanna spook them.'

They both continued to watch the advancing Griffins approach the church and towards Cleese, and they were amazed when they suddenly came to a stop after he ordered them to. For a few seconds the Griffins stood motionless in front of the outstretched arms of Cleese standing in the doorway of the church, they then went down onto the ground and paid homage to the great wizard.

'What is going on?' asked Mr P. 'I think they think that Cleese is some sort of god!'

'No,' replied Gertie, 'not a god — a wizard. It's like he has them under his spell. Look? He is getting them to stand.'

She was right, Cleese was moving his arms in an upright motion and the herd of Griffins began to rise up from their worship positions. Mr P could see the face of Cleese and he didn't seem to look fazed in any way like this was the most natural thing in the world for him to do.

This came as no surprise to Mr P; he always felt that his good friend was meant for bigger and greater things. He remembered back to a time when they were both studying at the revered order and Cleese was able to hypnotise the sacred owl and commanded it to defecate on the head of the grandmaster of judgements. To this day only Cleese and Mr P and a green haired female Willybum called Smosatek knew the truth — Cleese was in love with Smosatek but she broke his heart when she ran off with the guitarist in a semi-successful rock band.

But on this day, and in this timeline, Cleese was in his element. He turned around and walked back into the church, an action that resulted in the Griffins swiftly turning round and running back off to where they had presumably come from. Gertie was speechless. She knew that Mr P thought that Cleese was a real wizard, and certainly Cleese thought he was, but this was actual proof.

As the Griffins were out of sight Mr P and Gertie ran towards the church door and entered. 'Dude!' shouted Mr P. 'You are an actual wizard.'

'Yes, I know,' answered Cleese as he turned around to face his friends. 'And this is where I belong, I can feel it, this feels like the most natural thing in the whole world.'

Mr P had sympathy for Cleese, he had finally found his place in the existence of time and space, but unfortunately it wasn't in the time and place where he was born and lived.

'Cleese, we need to go, dude, anything could happen and then we may get stuck here,' said Mr P, but Cleese did not look concerned. He sat on a step to the side of the alter and looked cheerfully in the eyes of his two old friends.

'I'm staying here,' he said, 'this is where I belong. I've known it my whole life. I cannot go back to my old life knowing that this is where I need to be. They think I'm the wizard Merlin… and so do I.'

'But can you exist here?' asked Gertie.

'Yes, I just know it; it feels so natural I can't explain it. I just know that an instinct inside of me is telling me to stay.'

'Mate,' chipped in Mr P, 'we may not be able to come back for you. If you stay here then that is it.'

'I know, I'm gonna be OK, P,' Cleese answered. 'You two need to go.'

Cleese walked over to Mr P and Gertie and put his arms around them both. All three stood there lost in the moment knowing that this is the last time they are going to see each other.

'Babe, we need to go,' Gertie said, breaking the moment.

She pulled Mr P by the hand and led him to the place that they had arrived in earlier that day. She could tell that this was hard for him, the two of them had been inseparable friends for many years and this was the end.

As they approached the travel point Mr P stopped and took one last look at his great friend. 'So long, Merlin,' he said bowing his head. 'May you live in all eternity.'

There was a silence as Mr P and Gertie then proceeded to walk through the exit and disappeared leaving the great wizard Merlin to make history and create mythologies that will live forever.

It had been only a few seconds after they had entered through the secret door, did Mr P and Gertie come back out to where Ivan and Geoffrey were waiting.

'Where is Cleese?' asked Geoffrey.

'He ain't coming back, Doug,' answered Mr P. 'It was incredible, he… he just became aware of his place and chose to stay.'

Geoffrey took this remarkably well, but considering the circumstances, nothing was a surprise any more.

Mr P pulled the notebook and green crayon from his pocket and wrote:

The meaning of life — 7) Be authentic

'So he has found himself,' Geoffrey stated. Mr P and Gertie nodded.

Ivan gave a wry smile. He knew already.

The enormous bouncy castle of destiny

On planet Luyden b, there is a theme park with the biggest bouncy castle in the known universe, where hundreds upon hundreds of Dinglewits gather daily to bounce up and down and enjoy the feeling of bouncing. It was here, two thousand years ago, that the grand leader of the science department developed the Very Fast Engine (VFE), and thus, intergalactic travel was born. The first thing that the Dinglewits did with this new technology was to invade a distant planet, because they had some rather pretty looking stones that could be moulded into decorative ornaments and sold for profit. It soon became obvious however that this was not necessarily the best use of this amazing piece of machinery, even though the money was good, and so they began scouting the universe looking for new species and making friends.

On one of the first pioneering flights was a low-ranking officer who was the great grandfather of the one and only Mr P — he was also called Mr P — and it was he who made the fateful decision to settle on planet Earth and breed with a fellow Dinglewit called Beatrice. It was this decision that allowed for the continuation of the Mr P bloodline because, had he not chosen to stay on Earth, he would have been killed in the Orion wars along with the rest of the crew on board the star ship Galacticus.

The Orion wars were a terrible tragedy for all concerned and to this day no one really understands why it all started. Some say it was because of the VFE and that, due to the Dinglewits unwilling to share their invention, it made other species twitchy, while others claim that it was always going to happen because of Dinglewit nature and that it was only a matter of time before something happened. All we do know is that the population of Dinglewits, and of that of other species, was reduced dramatically and the positive effect that the VFE afforded had been potentially lost. The Dinglewits of Earth were lucky and escaped this disaster, as no one believed that the Earth had anything of any value that is worth fighting over. And so, they playfully went about their lives unattached to the devastation that was happening in the rest of the universe and the many species that lived within it. Thus, the Dinglewits on planet Earth are the friendliest species in the whole galaxy and Mr P and Gertie epitomised this to the extreme.

'Have you ever wanted to travel to the outer planets of Orion, babe?' Gertie asked Mr P as they both sat drinking their Jamaican Blue Mountain morning coffee. Since their meeting with Frisby they had managed to source the blend of amazing tasty coffee, but due to its price, only afforded themselves the luxury first thing in the morning — and possibly when relatives visit.

'Actually, I have,' answered Mr P. 'I have never said this to anyone before, but I have always wanted to travel to the Arushan planets. Apparently, the plants and the lakes and the insects on those planets are mind blowing. They say that at night the plants are luminescent and they sway in the wind and make magical sounds as they sway. It always seemed like paradise to me. I have always wanted to go there but I'm afraid that once I was there I wouldn't want to leave.'

Gertie smiled ruefully because she knew that if Mr P was to find meaning to his life then finding peace and happiness where you live is important, but she was also confused by his answer.

'Why would you be afraid to leave if you found paradise? Isn't that what we all seek?' she asked.

This was a good question thought Mr P, he hadn't really contemplated it before but Gertie was right, seeking paradise to live in is a quest for life. Birds will migrate and travel across vast continents and have to set up a completely new nest just to abandon it later in the year, fish will swim long distances to spawn before returning to their original waters, butterflies will migrate through three generations using only natural instinct in order to seek their journey's end, all to find their version of paradise. This got Mr P thinking about his own situation. He had always enjoyed living on Earth and had politely declined on a few occasions the opportunity to return to Luyten b, mainly because of the war, but where he lived on earth had always felt underwhelming. It suddenly occurred to Mr P that striving to have a better standard of living, whatever you defined as living, was an important factor in the meaning of life.

His ancestors had travelled through light years of cold space to find a better existence, and maybe, he had become a sea squirt that had settled for the easy life instead of looking for improvement. Or maybe he is living his best life and this is as good as it gets, and that, he didn't want to be the sort of Dinglewit that was constantly working for a better life without appreciating the one he had.

'Do you think we should go one day Gertie?' asked Mr P hoping that the answer was yes.

Gertie was all too happy to reciprocate. 'Yes, we should go, but not one day, let's arrange it now? Let's live for the "now" and not the "one-day"!'

Wow! thought Mr P, this was a change in roles, normally it's him that has the hair-brained ideas and it's Gertie that is the sensible one. He had unleashed the animal inside of her and now she is unstoppable. Normally she is only this determined when it comes to booking holidays. But nevertheless he liked it and so now they were going travelling, and not just travelling, but travelling the paradise planets of Arusha.

Timelines explained

Mr P was missing his old mate Cleese dearly. A spliff-fuelled afternoon in the garden isn't quite the same without your best mate talking shit at you and constantly falling over. His favourite conversation about how he is the world's greatest wizard — that used to wear thin at the time — is now the very thing that he missed about him. And he would love to pick him up off the floor and sweep up the broken glass one last time.

Geoffrey was a good friend but they never had the connection that he had with Cleese. He knew that one of the things that gave purpose and meaning to your life is being around Dinglewits that you like. But I guess all great things must come to an end he thought, and if one good thing comes out of the end of the LPMD, then him and Gertie and Mya travelling to the Arusha planets is not a bad outcome.

The Arushan planets are a long way away and it would take many months to get there. Not only that but the path that they need to travel was heavily affected by the Orion wars, and thus, are very dangerous. But with their plans finalised and their focus on the journey ahead they boarded their new space ship — the Pretty Flamingo — and made themselves at home. The

Flamingo is a medium sized vessel designed for comfortable long trips to distant planets. There is ample room in the cargo bay for Logey the campervan and the accommodation are very comfortable. They were able to buy the Pretty Flamingo with the money they raised from the sale of Hunters Lodge and that gave them plenty of funds in reserve. They are well stashed for the journey and they don't really need to stop off anywhere for supplies but if they find a safe place then they will consider it in order to preserve their sanity and before cabin fever sets in.

And so once again, with everything packed, they are embarking on another adventure, but this time it's to find their dream home. Many had taken this arduous journey before them and there had been mixed reviews, but like everywhere else, if you have money, you should be fine.

The Pretty Flamingo left Earth on a drizzly morning. There had been some trepidation about the route that the navigation system plotted as the computer seemed unaware of the need for regular stops at safe havens. But with a bit of re-adjustment the stops were planned and the adventure began.

As with all great journeys the initial excitement began with singing and a general good vibe and the Pretty Flamingo could have been mistaken for a party ship. Gertie and Mya are singing songs on the radio and Mr P is busy doing blue jobs. In the background the Earth is beginning to fade and grow smaller in size.

They quickly pass the Musk telescope and get very excited as they see the dark side of the moon for the first time. Gertie states that it looks just like the light side of the moon — only darker. Mr P agrees and shows his disappointment with the inevitable anti-climax that can be assigned to most of the wonders of the universe. They once went on holiday to Cereus and that was just awful, in fact Gertie went home early after developing a funny bottom as she calls it, quickly followed by Mr P.

It doesn't take too long before they reach the underwater planet of Europa where they can relax and see the giant sea creatures that have lived there for millions of years. This is a pleasant surprise to Mr P and Gertie, as they hadn't expected too much from a giant aquarium, because all the ones they had visited on Earth were rubbish. But this one was better. Here they sat and ate lunch while watching giant Leedsichthys eat vast amounts of sea fodder and watched with awe as Livyatans scoured their territory looking for a mate. This was much better than Earth aquariums.

Their journey had started well. Mya is enjoying the adventure and Gertie is looking as relaxed as she had ever been. 'We could just stay here, babe,' she said while resting back into her seat. 'We can both get jobs and enjoy looking at these beautiful sea monsters forever.'

Mr P wasn't having any of this. 'We would soon get bored of this, Gertie. No, we must keep moving.'

But this got Mr P thinking. Was Gertie right to suggest that they stay there? It must happen all the time where a destination is sought but along the way a place of tranquillity is found and so the journey ends. The fun of an adventure is, after all, the actual journey itself, and that doesn't necessarily mean that the initial end-point becomes the only acceptable outcome. And if by starting on that journey to the Arushan planets meant that they discovered another equally gorgeous place then so be it. That said, this was not that gorgeous place and so after a couple of days of rest they were back in the Pretty Flamingo and heading out into deep space.

Now the Orion wars had left a massive scar on the fabric of the universe, and by that, I mean the actual fabric of space, the underlying energy that holds all matter and anti-matter together had, sort of, giant holes in them caused by powerful lasers and neutron bombs. Many ships over the past few years had wandered into these holes within the fabric of space-time never to be seen again. It is not known whether they had been transported to another dimension in space, or even transported to another dimension in time, or even both as space and time are mysteriously linked. But one thing was for sure, these holes are to be avoided at all costs. Most have now been surveyed and pin-pointed onto a map that can be bought in any good book shop, and most even have a lighthouse situated near them to warn travellers of their whereabouts. No, getting sucked into a hole in space would be bad news. As a result, the journey from Europa to their next stop had to be via the asteroid cloud of Morgaine that, in itself, is a perilous excursion. While on their travels Gertie had plenty of time to contemplate the past events.

'I've been thinking, babe,' she said, as the Pretty Flamingo left Europa bound for the asteroid cloud. 'Cleese is now Merlin — the legendary wizard from history and a significant player in Arthurian legend — and we were also there, so are we characters from history? Because, if you read up on this then I could be the lady of the lake who gave the Holy Grail to Lancelot, because I did. And if this is so then I am also part of the Arthurian Legend. And if that is the case then we are an essential part of history that is on a loop in time.'

Mr P looked around from his position in the front seat of the Pretty Flamingo where he was monitoring the self-drive systems.

'Can you see where I'm coming from?' she continued. 'If this is true then time is not as we thought and the arrow of time that normally points forward is, in fact, more of a circle of a figure of eight or something like that.'

Mr P got up from his seat and walked over to the dining table where there was a pen and paper upon it.

'Is it a figure eight, or is it more like an elongated letter e?' and with that he began to draw.

B

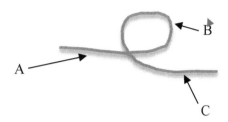

After which he started to label his drawing. 'Well, I think it's like this, babe,' Mr P explained. 'The letter A is the original time line that we all start on, then B is us going back in time and A C interacting with the original passage of time, and then C is the new passage of time. What do you think of that?'

'Well,' answered Gertie, 'if that is the case then what happens to line A after we interfere and make changes?'

'Nothing happens to it, Gertie,' Mr P answered. 'Some Dinglewits think that it continues and that there becomes lots of alternative time lines but that doesn't make sense. No. Once the timeline has been changed then it has been changed and C becomes the timeline. Nothing else makes any sense.'

'But what if we hadn't gone back in time and made the changes then A would simply have carried on and the Holy Grail would not have been given to Lancelot and Merlin would not have existed. But we know that

that all happened because we read about it before we did it,' Gertie deduced.

'Exactly, Gertie! And the reason we read about it is because we did go back and make the changes,' Mr P answered.

'But that means that life is mapped out in and that we are not free to make our own decisions,' said Gertie. And she didn't much enjoy saying that either as she always believed in free will.

'No, it doesn't, babe, not necessarily,' Mr P added. 'You see we read about it because we did make the decision to go back, if we hadn't then it wouldn't have happened and we wouldn't have read about it. It's not that our lives have been mapped out it's just that we had already made the decision before we even knew that we had. Cleese was always Merlin, and if we are to be honest, it's pretty obvious now that he was. He always said that he was a reincarnation of Merlin but in fact he was actually Merlin himself. This is how life is. When you have a sense of deja-vu it just means that you have been there before or that someone has changed the timeline and has affected you in some little way.'

Gertie interrupted. 'Or even that you were there before someone changed history by entering the timeline and changing it so you are just visiting the same place that you would have done but slightly delayed because of the changes.'

'That's spot on, I reckon, Gertie,' Mr P answered. 'All these changes that we feel are just fluctuations in the arrow of time as it loops over to restart because someone has changed it. It makes sense to me.'

'And me!' Gertie replied.

Suddenly the lights turned red and the Pretty Flamingo issued a verbal warning. 'Warning! Warning! Goliaths are in the vicinity, I repeat, Goliaths are in the vicinity.'

This meant trouble. A Goliath can eat the the Pretty Flamingo in one gulp and there would be little escape if it did. Mr P ran down to the control centre and sat in the pilot's seat. Now under normal circumstances this is a very cool thing to do. The pilot's seat is bright red in colour and is able to swivel around and move with just the slightest movement of the pilot. It is not attached to either the floor or the ceiling; instead, it uses a magnetic force to keep it in its natural position. This allows for a super soft suspension when things get bumpy, and that could be appropriate for what is about to happen.

Mr P quickly put the headgear on and switched the controls from autopilot to manual. He was now in control of the the Pretty Flamingo and put everyone's lives in his hands. He shouted through the small cabin door. 'Gertie, Gertie, I need your help with navigation.' Gertie ran up the hallway towards the cockpit.

'I've strapped Mya into the escape pod just in case,' she quickly blurted out.

Now asking Gertie to navigate was something that Mr P did not do lightly. She is notorious for being absolutely useless at navigation but that mainly to do with day dreaming and forgetting when to turn. Mr P hoped that her concentration would be maintained due to the gravity of the situation, but he couldn't be 100% sure.

As Mr P looked out of the cockpit window, he could see lots and lots of rocks. They weren't too close together and under normal speed even he could find a path through them. However, at high speeds this task would become very tricky indeed.

'Babe, can you plot me a route through the rocks where we can travel at high speeds, I don't really want to be making too many sharp turns?'

'Okey-dokey, Captain,' came the sarcastic reply. Mr P raised his eyelids and shook his head. He began to speed up in preparation for the presence of the Goliaths.

'There!' shouted Gertie, 'a Goliath to the right coming right at us.'

Mr P turned, the Pretty Flamingo to the left and squeezed full throttle. The Pretty Flamingo shuddered as if to blow the smoke out of its exhaust then began speeding up. The Goliath took chase. It was huge, but by the standards of a Goliath, it was considered a baby. Even so it could easily devour the Pretty Flamingo in one easy guzzle, and Mr P had no intention of being a tasty aperitif for the ugly slug looking flying dragon type space creature. No, he was not. He swerved through a couple of rocks and turned right in order to shake off the dastardly beast, then quickly upwards, but this did not shake the Goliath of their tails.

'Babe,' shouted Gertie, 'take a left then another quick left and head towards that cluster over there.'

'Are you sure we can get through it?' answered Mr P as he followed her orders while at the same time increasing the speed of the Pretty Flamingo.

'No, we can't get through it,' Gertie replied, 'but it might make the Goliath scared.'

'EHHHH,' said Mr P in a panicky voice, 'we are trying to out-run the thing not make it scared.'

'Oh,' Gertie replied. 'Oh, sorry. OK, leave it with me.'

Mr P was frantically looking from side to side as they hastily headed towards the cluster of rocks followed closely by the Goliath.

'It ain't working, babe, it ain't getting scared,' he shouted to Gertie, while simultaneously whispering, 'but I am,' to himself. The cluster of rocks drew ever closer as the speed of the Pretty Flamingo increased.

'Any news on a route out yet, babe?' Mr P continued. He knew there was no point in putting her under too much pressure as she will just clam up and so needs to tread carefully.

'Just keep going I'm working on it,' she replied.

Now Goliaths are known for being very aggressive when anything enters their territory, and just like most primitive creatures, will do all in its path to defend his area, and it appears that they had wandered right into the middle of its territory. The speed of the Pretty Flamingo was able to keep the Goliath off its tail for now but the deep space sea slug was slowly making ground. Fifty metres — forty-five metres — forty metres — the Goliath was beginning to catch them up. One detail that is known about Goliaths is that they are not very nimble and require a big turning circle. This is due mainly to them being forward runners that can generate vast speeds by flapping their back wings, however, they have nothing to the side and no way of generating force in a sideways direction, so a quick turn easily evades them. But they soon catch up.

'Any idea yet, babe?' asked Mr P.

'Errr, just turn right I guess,' Gertie replied.

'Oh, just turn right I guess,' Mr P whispered, he was starting to have second thoughts about letting Gertie be in charge of navigation. But having no other options he turned right. This shook off the Goliath for a few seconds while it slowed and turned around. However, they were now heading towards a lighthouse.

'BAAABE, we are heading towards a hole in space,' Mr P hollered over to Gertie. 'Left or right?'

'Left,' came the reply. 'No, err, yeah left, definitely left.'

The Goliath was gaining ground, and with no other options, Mr P closed his eyes and turned left, straight towards another Goliath. Mr P took a big sigh and puffed out his cheeks, this was typical of Gertie's navigational skills and he should have known better. Now they had two Goliaths wanting to eat them. The creature in front of them looked different.

'It's a female,' shouted Gertie, and with that huge brightly coloured wing like flaps sprang out of her neck and made a glorious peacock-like display.

It was hard not to be impressed by this show of courtship and Mr P smiled as he headed towards his doom. But rather than eating them the female Goliath simply let them fly by to safety. She had other things on her mind , and as they flew underneath the horny love monster, the Goliath that had been chasing them slowed and began flirt with it.

'Ahhh,' shouted Gertie, 'we are match-makers, look babe, they are getting it on.'

Mr P looked in the rear-view camera and could see a very strange mating ritual that he cared not to see, and in fact would have been quite happy had he never seen it in his whole lifetime. But he was happy to be alive , and as Gertie came over and sat on his lap and completely distracted him with a big sloppy kiss, they flew through a space hole.

'Oh bugger!' said Mr P.

Traversable wormholes and the Polchinski paradox

Some things are really important when talking about wormholes. Firstly, they are a great method for travelling vast distances instantaneously — if you can figure out where the other end is — and secondly, some have the ability to travel through the dimensions of time — but again if you get the right wormhole. The major drawback to wormhole travelling is that they are extremely unstable, so they can't be relied upon to offer a long-term solution to intergalactic space travel. The longest surviving known wormhole in the universe has been stable for over five thousand years however and was used extensively during the Orion wars, whereas some wormholes will exist for a matter of milliseconds. There have been many reports of ships mysteriously disappearing into instantly formed and collapsing wormholes where the ship and its crew are never seen or heard of again. An area of space known as the Roman Arch is notorious for these kinds of phenomena and often a cargo ship will avoid an area if it is known to have these Clegg' holes.

Traverse wormholes are particularly useful for intergalactic travel as they offer a route back and forth from a particular area of space-time and many wormholes that have been flagged and had a lighthouse placed at its entrance are traverse wormholes. Entire civilisations have sprung up around the entrance to such marvels and act as outposts and colonies to super massive empires.

The Dinglewit civilisation emerged from such an empire and thus the influence of the inhabitants of Luyten b benefitted from technologies and knowledge of higher developed species and was able to dominate their particular corner of the universe. The big problem with this however was that their civilisation was too immature to understand what to do with the technology they had gained — without the structure of which to discover it for themselves — and so misused the technology for personal gain. This was the case for the universal web, a technology borrowed from the ancient humans after the great catastrophe of 2030 when artificial intelligence was given the power of national security and the command of their armies, and was used by the Dinglewits to suppress original and unruly thoughts.

The thought machine was sold to the population initially as a great resource for gaining knowledge and to make their lives easier, but it soon became apparent that it was also being used to manipulate the individual Dinglewit, but by this time it was too late, and the vast majority of Dinglewits lost the ability to make informed decisions based on their own personal feelings and experiences and so herd consciousness was lost.

Anyway, back to wormholes. The Polchinski paradox examines the potential for an object to interfere with itself by colliding with itself when entering a space-time wormhole.

Was this the case here?

Had somehow in the future Mr P and Gertie entered a Polchinski wormhole and interfered with themselves?

Is this why Cleese knew he was Merlin?

And Gertie turned out to be the Lady of the Lake? Mr P wanted answers.

The Pretty Flamingo

A few seconds ago, Mr P, Gertie and Mya were being chased by a hungry Goliath looking for an easy meal, now they are in serene and empty space and with nothing in sight. Mr P leaned forward from the control stick and looked out the windows. He looked left, he looked right, he looked up, and he looked down. Nothing…

'Babe, where are we?' he asked.

Gertie quickly looked at the navigation system and scratched her head. Apart from the question from Mr P it was totally silent inside the Pretty Flamingo. The excitement of the last few minutes had waned and now they seemed lost in space. Prior to leaving the Earth their journey had been mapped out, their route being meticulously planned to include rest breaks, and even hotels booked to provide entertainment. This was supposed to be a road trip to the outer planets of the Milky Way, not a magical mystery tour party set adrift in the middle of bloody nowhere. Gertie continued to scour the map for an approximate location. There were a few planets in their vicinity but nothing that she could recognise, and certainly nothing that resembled a living planet.

'Baaaabe, where are we?' Mr P asked again.

'I don't know,' came the reply that nobody wanted to hear.

Mr P looked at Gertie, then looked at Mya. 'Mya go and take a bath while me and Mummy sort this out.'

'OK, Daddy,' she gleefully replied. Mya did not seem troubled by the events and was happily singing to herself as she left the control pod, but then again Mya was always in a world of her own. She had learned many years ago that everything would turn out just fine when she is with her parents, and so she skipped off singing her favourite song.

Gertie however, did look concerned. 'I don't know where we are,' she mumbled. 'I don't know where we are.'

'Don't worry, babe,' replied Mr P, 'things always sort themselves out in the end. Something will come up.'

He walked over to where Gertie was sat and he put his arms around her neck and they both looked at the map. 'Do you know the names of these planets?' he asked.

'No, I've never seen them before,' Gertie replied. 'I'll ask the computer.'

Gertie began typing instructions to get the navigation computer to try and locate their location. This was not always straightforward as a lot of space was yet to be discovered and charted, and where they were, did not look at all familiar. Gertie finished typing in the question and they both sat and waited for the answer. This was taking longer than normal as if the computer was struggling to comprehend the answer it was about to give. They waited. And they waited, until finally the blank screen gave an answer.

Location: Laniakea — Virgo Supercluster — Milky Way Time: Pending…

'Well, that's just great!' sighed Mr P. 'So there are over 100 billion planets to choose from with about ten billion that are able to support life.'

He leaned over Gertie's shoulder and typed into the computer exact location in the Milky Way? The reply was simple.

Location: South of the Morgaine asteroid field.

Mr P and Gertie looked at each other in complete surprise. 'It's just taken us to the other side of the asteroid field, babe,' Gertie said in a joyful manner. 'We've just escaped from the Goliaths and now we can carry on with our journey.'

'I think not, Gertie,' Mr P replied, 'because if that is the case then where is the Casio military base? It should be here, but it isn't.'

Gertie's draw dropped open, she knew Mr P was right and moved her head closer to the screen and looked for signs of the military base. The Casio military base was set up to protect this part of the Orion Arm from the invading tribes of the Murray Clans that operated out of Andromeda.

The Murray Clans were a very mobile tribe that began the Orion wars with their insistence on having the interstellar death-ray gun that the Dinglewits on planet Luyten b acquired from their meetings with the Zimmer Empire. The Zimmer Empire developed this weapon but had never used it on another species, as they knew that the main benefit of it was to act as a deterrent, and to prevent major planets from going to war in the first place. Being a benevolent bunch however, as well as understanding the psychology of fear, the Zimmer Empire gladly shared the weapon with their potential enemies in order to ensure a status quo. This was something that the Dinglewits did not understand and so, when the Murray Clan felt threatened by the existence of this weapon, the Dinglewits simply used it on the Clans as a warning not to mess with them. Inevitably this led to a local conflict that, through friendship treaties, eventually amounted to all-out war. Now the Zimmer Empire had good intentions when they gave the technology over to the Dinglewits as this is something they had always done to prevent a war, but what they didn't understand was that the Dinglewits were not ready for this type of military capability, and so defended their perceived advantage with all their might. This, of course, is a natural instinct of survival that eventually changes as the civilisation evolves, but

193

the civilisation DOES need the time to evolve. When any civilisation is forced into social change that they are not naturally ready for then conflict almost inevitably follows.

Boomer

Anyway, back to the story. Mr P and Gertie had spent the last ten minutes looking around the outside of the Pretty Flamingo in a vain attempt to see the military base that should be there, but it wasn't. This was a mystery as the station used to be a massive military station comparable to a small city. The amount of people living there supported an entire economy and there were generations of families and businesses associated with it. So why had it suddenly been disbanded and completely disappeared? This was strange.

Mr P stopped the Pretty Flamingo and looked at Gertie. 'Babe,' he said in an authoritative tone, 'suit up we are going outside.'

'Bugger that!' came the reply, Gertie had done a spacewalk before and she was not about to squeeze into another tight-fitting suit and feel claustrophobic again.

'No, you go, I will stay here and look for evidence,' she said in an equally authoritative tone.

This decision didn't come as a surprise to Mr P, or anyone that knows Gertie for that matter, and so he clambered down the very tight space that the ladder uses to enter into the cargo bay.

Although the Pretty Flamingo was not a particularly large spaceship, the ladder was longer than you would have expected, and it took Mr P some considerable effort to scale down to the bottom.

The cargo bay was dark but there were glimpses of light emerging through the spaces between the piles of boxes that were stacked up in a random manner. The space suits are situated in the right-hand corner of the cargo bay where they sit proudly reflecting in the window that is now overseeing the darkness of space. Mr P's suit was navy blue with yellow sleeves and the last time he wore it was on a weekend to trip to Venus when Gertie fell into a lake and he urinated into it because he was laughing so much. Mr P was confident that he had it cleaned but he wasn't 100% sure.

The suit fitted perfectly and as he opened the outside hatch door, he felt a tremendous sense of freedom. He stepped out onto the patio area near the hatch door and slowly walked over to the edge of the seating area and looked out into the void. Nothing. He looked left and right. He looked up and down. This is so peculiar he thought, nothing can explain the disappearance of the Casio station, and if it did leave, what happened to the surrounding structures. Mr P stood motionless with his hands on his hips pondering the question when there became a sudden smell of urine. Mr P turned up his nose and looked alarmingly at his crotch region. He was sure that he had it cleaned but the stench was awful. As he ventured further along the

Pretty Flamingo he could see a small moving object hopping around on the outside of the ship. It was fluffy with a massive beak and looked about the size of a big rabbit.

'Can you see this, Gertie?' Mr P asked through the communication headset, 'it looks like a Marsh Boomer.'

He walked closer to the prancing creature. 'What's it doing all way out here? Surely it can't have survived the journey through the wormhole.'

'Babe, catch it, babe, catch it!' Gertie shrieked. 'It is a Marsh Boomer, argh catch it, babe, catch it.'

Mr P crept over to the fluffy space pet with his hands out straight. He slowly got to his knees and gently crawled towards the now sitting, Marsh Boomer. 'Koochy Koo — Koochy Koo,' said Mr P, 'come to daddy.'

Mr P quickly lunged forward and tried to grab the Boomer but unfortunately it was way too quick for him and speedily ran round to the other side of the ship. Mr P gave chase running as fast as he could considering he was in zero gravity and handicapped with a clumsy space suit, but the Boomer would not be caught. Round and round they ran for over ten minutes until Mr P was laid on his back gasping for breath. He was breathing so fast and deep that his visor began to steam up.

'You OK, babe?' asked Gertie concerned that Mr P could barely string a sentence together.

'I think I need a couple of bellows,' came the exhausted response. Just at that moment the face of an ugly fluffy Marsh Boomer put its face right up to Mr P's helmet visor and began licking it. The Boomer then stood on Mr P's chest as if he now owned the Dinglewit and claimed him as his pet. Mr P put his arms around the Boomer and gingerly got up from his supine position and headed back into the Pretty Flamingo's cargo bay door to find Gertie waiting to claim their new pet.

'It's beautiful,' she said with a glint in her eye, 'we are keeping it. Come here, Boom Boom, come to Mummy?'

'It's a girl,' Mr P added. 'What shall we call her?'

'Boomer, we are calling her Boomer,' Gertie answered immediately. She then grabbed Boomer off Mr P and took their new family pet into the warmth of the Pretty Flamingo to be forever mollycoddled.

The evening meal was eaten and still Mr P and Gertie were none the wiser about the events of the day. Boomer had settled in and was asleep in a makeshift bed after eating a whole chicken and drunk two bowls of water. Mr P was sat in a domed glass room looking out at the stars of the Milky Way and admiring its beauty. It's rare to see the stars like this when living on Earth due to the light pollution, but up here they can be seen in all their glory.

Gertie entered the room quietly and put her arms around Mr P and whispered, 'I've figured it out!'

Mr P turned around.

Gertie continued, 'We have gone back in time! It's the only explanation, because we cannot go forward in time, so we must have entered a wormhole that has sent us back in time. Otherwise, everything would still be here. Yes, we have definitely gone back in time.'

'But we can go forward in time, babe,' stated Mr P, 'we have done it before.'

'No, we haven't,' Gertie replied. 'We have only gone back to a time that we started from. We have never gone forwards beyond the arrow of time of which we are in. No, we can only go back to a place in history then return to our natural time. So if the Casio station isn't here then we have gone back to a time before it was built.'

This made sense to both of them, and the mood suddenly changed. They both knew what this meant. They were potentially lost in time, and a time that they knew nothing about nor belonged to. But being a let's live in the moment type of people they decided not to let it ruin their day. Mr P decided to walk Boomer around the Pretty Flamingo and do some thinking. Gertie opened a bottle of cheap Saturnian red wine and caught up on her soaps.

As Mr P and Boomer were walking the abandoned corridors of the old creaking ship a thought began to enter his head. The good thing about being in history is that you know where everything is and what is about to happen, he thought to himself. For example, he knew when and why the Orion wars began, he knew when humans abandoned Earth for the desolate planet of Proxima Centauri, and he knew that he might be able to change some of these events and prevent future catastrophes. I could leave clues for the inhabitants of the planets and warn them of their impending doom he thought and he could make the universe a better place to live. He reached into his pocket and pulled out his notebook and green crayon

The meaning of life — 8) Improve your world.

Yes, he thought. One of the meanings of life must be to enhance the world around you and leave it a better place than when you found it. This conclusion made Mr P happy. Like Gertie, they had always felt a sense of well-being when doing good things for others, and now, perhaps, they could do the ultimate good deed and prevent a generation of misery. A tall order perhaps, but a worthy one.

'Boomer,' said Mr P to the now, family pet. 'I think we have a meaning to our lives, we are going to leave markers to warn against the stupidity of all living creatures against the perils of their potential future. What do you think? Will this work?'

Of course Boomer had no idea what was happening and instead chose to continue sniffing around the space ship. This continued for quite some time until Mr P decided enough was enough and headed back to the main living area. It was starting to look like home now. Gertie had painted as few walls and hung a couple of pictures, and Mya had made some cushions of her own design that complemented the overall ambience.

'Do we know when in time it is, Gertie?' asked Mr P. 'Can't we tell by the formation of the constellations or something? Because if we know when it is then we can tell what was happening in the universe at that time and possibly help to nurture it in the right direction.'

'Wow!' answered Gertie. 'You have been thinking ain't ya. I reckon having a Marsh Boomer as a pet has been good for you. Let me find out when in time we are.' Gertie walked over to the control panel and looked to see if the "pending" had ended. It had. It now read

Time: Luyten b — 20,00 YoE (years of existence)
Earth — 200 AD

'Excellent,' shouted Mr P. 'We now know when we are.'

He ran into the small library situated to the rear of the Pretty Flamingo and started flicking through encyclopaedias and other ancient texts that would offer a clue to their new situation. Gertie chose to leave it with him as she had some soaps to catch up on. He spent all night scouring the old and dusty pages of the books that had been sold with the space ship as no one reads words on parchment any more as it is deemed very old fashioned indeed. But Mr P loved a book. For him there was something special about holding a book in his hand and flicking through the printed pages in the hope of finding something interesting. Dinglewits had long given up this pursuit instead opting to tap into the universal web for their knowledge that is automatically transferred into the brains as a memory. Mr P was always sceptical of this form of learning as it was very open to censorship and propaganda. He was one of the few Dinglewits that collected books, and indeed, the few that he had accumulated during his short life was now part of the collection on board the Pretty Flamingo. This interest in books had led him to know all about the ancient libraries that ever existed in the universe, like the great library of Alexandria in the times of the ancient Earth, or the superior library of Angar on the planet of Cedar. The Cedar library was always a dream for Mr P but as it was destroyed by the Orion wars that dream looked like it was never to be, until now. Now all was possible. You see Mr P and Gertie now live in a time before the devastation so they are able to visit and see the sites that had been consigned to the history books. Great waterfalls that are now dry, or forests that had been destroyed, or cultures that thrived within their own existence before being removed and replaced. Gertie had always shown an interest in visiting ancient India in the early days of the Earth when humans occupied it, particularly as she loved the food that came from that era. Mr P, however, was more interested in books and he now had his heart set on going to Cedar to visit the superior library.

Bloody Einstein

There was once a very clever human called Albert Einstein, and he came up with a few answers to some of the big questions of the day. One of his ideas was the concept of space-time as a theory to explain the movement of planets moving through space. Mr P liked this theory and had always bought into it.

Until now!

Sat in his observatory on board the Pretty Flamingo, Mr P was starting to question the whole concept of space-time as a means of understanding the universe. This is because he had now seen for himself a lot more than even Einstein could ever comprehend. The big thing for Mr P was the existence of living creatures. You see, to Mr P, time is a concept that was invented by living creatures to calculate the direction of entropy. But entropy can be altered by the impact that living creatures have upon it. Therefore, for a theory to be complete it has to involve and explain the input of the living. Otherwise, it can always be interfered with and altered and thus the equations will never work out. So now that the space-time continuum theory had been debunked Mr P needed a new one. Unfortunately, he wasn't clever enough to think of it himself but perhaps he could use his crumpet theory as a basis.

For those who may have forgotten, the crumpet theory imagined space as layers of edible foodstuffs with holes in. The holes allowed for travel between the different layers (or dimensions) of existence, and looks just like a crumpet. In reality the holes in the crumpets are wormholes and to travel between the layers of the crumpet one need simply drive into the wormhole and voilà.

As a theory it was weak, but considering what Mr P had seen and experienced recently, it was beginning to make sense.

To make an equation for such a theory was beyond the brainpower of Mr P. For that he needed a genius, but geniuses are hard to come by these days. Once he got to the superior library of Angar on the planet Cedar perhaps he could find a genius there to do the maths for him.

For now though, he will just call it the space-time-life continuum.

The Great Library

The remainder of the journey to the planet Cedar passed without event and they parked the Pretty Flamingo at a carport on the outside of Angar city. They took the park and ride into the centre. The city was a hive of activity. Since the revolution the planet had become a safe refuge for all life forms, and it was one of the few places where Dinglewits could mix with Langtons, and where Willybums lived side by side with Lurchers. That is not to say that life was easy or safe. No, in fact there were still tensions between the different species that occasionally spilled over into unrest. But for the most part they learned to get along and share the freedoms that Cedar offered.

While in the city the plan was for Gertie and Mya to go shopping at the Bullmarket, a clothes shop adored by women, for the large amount of cheap tat, while Mr P visited the Superior library of Angar to discover the meaning of life. They were to meet up at the café across the road when they had finished.

At the corner of 23rd Street they kissed and went their separate ways. For the first time in months Mr P had some time to himself and he liked it. A grin appeared on his face as he walked up to the entrance of the library where he stood and marvelled at the huge revolving doors. They were at least ten metres tall and made of glass. They revolved quite fast for such a large structure, but hordes and hordes of scholars and readers, were only too happy to squeeze through them as they spun around. As many came out of the doors as went in , and at one point, Mr P thought that they were just going round and round and not actually entering the building at all. But of course they were. He stood in line, happily with a warm feeling in one of his two hearts, waiting for his turn to run in through the revolving glass doors. This was a dream come true, but he wished that Gertie was there to share it with him. That took some of the edge off. But hey-ho, it is what it is, and as he ran through the revolving doors and entered into the lobby, he could see a grand staircase directly in front of him. The hustle and bustle of outside was now replaced by a feeling of calm. Hanging down from the tall ceilings were two enormous glass candelabras. They were the main source of light for the lobby and everyone that entered looked up at them in awe. They were a gift to the library from the imperial leader of Luyten b, and thus, every Dinglewit in the universe was always very welcome within the library walls.

The Great Library of Angar is unique in the fact that the planet of Cedar is situated within a time vortex. The product of this being that every book that has ever been written, or ever will be written, is here. There are books from the ancient past right up until the end of the universe. All here under one roof. One gigantic roof. Every language, whether written in text form or coded into sound waves, every fictional topic and every factual textbook, all here under the splendour of the giant candelabras at the Superior library of Angar. The biggest section is, of course, psychology. And that is the psychology of everything ranging from human psychology to Hessian rodent psychology, regarded by many as being the most complicated of all personalities to comprehend due to the their three brains. The smallest section is German human comedy. Very slim pickings there.

Mr P made his way up the grand staircase looking all around as he walked. Everyone else was doing the same and as he got to the top of the first flight and onto the landing of the first floor he was confronted by another grand staircase. In fact, there was a grand staircase leading to every single floor of the twelve floors within the library. Mr P looked left and saw a never-ending corridor with rooms coming off both sides, he looked right and it was the same. This place is gigantic he thought to himself.

He stood at the top of the staircase not really knowing which way to turn, and as he stood there looking left and right, he thought bugger it and sat down on a fortunately placed sofa to give it some thought.

Within a flash of him sitting down a strange looking creature from, what could only be described as, the Empire of Freaky Looking Flat Heads sat next to him.

'Big innit?' said the stranger with a peculiar flat cranium and boggly eyes. 'This is my twelfth time here and I still can't get over how big it is, I've only visited two floors so far, and I'm determined to see 'em all. Oh, by the way my name is Po Olemit, they call me Mitty, it's nice to meet you.'

'Hello, Mitty. I'm Mr P and this is my first time here.'

'Mr P! Don't you have a first name?'

'Well, no, not really, my close friends call me P. But that is my name.'

'What species are you?' asked Mitty. 'You look like a Gorgovite.'

This surprised Mr P as Gorgovites had been extinct for centuries following the great mercury famine, which was their only source of food.

'I'm a Dinglewit, Mitty, we are from a planet about ten light years from here. I'm surprised you haven't heard of us, we are quite well travelled.'

'Oh yes that's right, Dinglewits, you are a long way from home. What are you doing here?'

'I'm here to seek the meaning to life. I think there must be a book here somewhere.'

'There is,' replied Mitty. 'In fact, there is a whole room dedicated to it. I haven't been there but it's on the eighth floor. I was planning on getting to it in about 300 years or so but I guess we could visit it now.'

'Three hundred years? How long do you live for may I ask?'

Mitty shrugged his shoulders. 'I don't know, no one does, it's a great mystery. That's why I'm here. To figure the whole thing out.'

'How long have you been coming here for?'

'I don't know that either, but every morning I wake up and I come here. It just feels like the right thing to do.'

'Don't you think that's a little strange?'

'Yes. Very.'

Mr P looked inquisitively at Mitty and gave a wry grin. 'Have you never thought about breaking the cycle?' he asked.

'Yes, many times,' answered Mitty, 'but it's just easier and less risky to keep coming here.'

Mr P knew how he felt. He had spent much of his life doing the safe and easy option. It just instinctively feels like the right thing to do.

'Well,' said Mr P, 'if it gets you through the day then keep doing it.'

Just then the whole of existence flickered and Mitty was gone. Mr P frantically looked around gobsmacked that anything could just disappear. But then as suddenly as he vanished Mitty was walking back up the grand staircase and back towards the sofa.

'Big innit?' said Mitty as he sat down next to Mr P — for the second time. 'This is my twelfth time here and I still can't get over how big it is. I've only visited two floors so far, and I'm determined to see 'em all. Oh, by the way, my name is Poolemit, they call me Mitty, it's nice to meet you.'

Mr P was amazed, while at the same time a little hurt, that Mitty hadn't remembered him. But he didn't have time for silly games that the universe was deciding to play. He felt sorry for Mitty, but he was busy, and besides, he seemed happy enough with his existence, so Mr P made his excuses and left. He found the lift and made his way to the eighth floor.

The eighth floor was much like all the rest. There was an endless corridor with an endless number of rooms on each side and at the top of each staircase their stood a lowly security guard sat on a chair staring forward.

Mr P approached the guard. 'Please, sir,' he asked. 'I'm looking for the meaning of life.'

'Oh, you as well, eh,' sighed the guard in a despondent manner. 'To the right, and the third room in,' he continued.

'Thanks, and err, have there been many looking for the meaning of life, then?' asked Mr P.

'About 100 a day use that room, but none of them leave with the answers they come looking for,' the guard replied. 'I don't know what they are expecting from them books but they never seemed satisfied.'

'Oh, well I will have to find out for myself then, I guess.'

'Yep.'

The conversation ended and Mr P walked off.

The room that was third on the right had a sign over the door at the entrance, it read:

"Enter all ye lost souls and leave a bit of your soul behind."

Mr P smirked as he read the sign but thought to himself that it was quite a sinister message to leave at the entrance to a library entrance. Or in fact, anywhere in a library. But undeterred he entered the room in high spirits.

The room was in sections, and there were lots of sections. There was a section on mortality, a section on death, a section on research (there is always a section on research), a section on love, and so on.

'This is no good to me,' said Mr P in a hushed tone and he continued to walk down the room looking at every section in turn. But nothing jumped out at him. Then, right at the very bottom in the bottom corner there was a very small section on "time".

Hmm he thought I wonder if Cleese is in there? He knelt down and quickly shuffled through the few books that were tightly crammed in. And there it was "Arthurian legends".

Mr P picked it up and stared at the front cover. There was Cleese as Merlin; there was Gertie as the Lady of the Lake, and there was himself, bang central, and holding Excalibur.

'Noooo,' he said out loud. He put the book to his chest and sat down on the floor. There were a few other life forms in the room and they looked rather unconcerned by the events that were taking place, and after a quick glimpse they carried on with their pre-arranged routine. A minute or more passed before Mr P managed to pluck up the courage to grasp the book with both hands and took another look.

It was him. Arthur.

I'm King Arthur he thought to himself. SHIT.

This changes everything. Does that mean I'm going to go back in time and free the Britons? Of course it does.

Oh shit.

He put the book under his armpit and ran out of the room, past the security guard who was still sat motionless looking in front of himself, down the grand staircases, and down in the direction of Mitty who, again was walking from the lobby and up the grand staircase to the first floor.

'Mitty, Mitty, come with me!' yelled Mr P at the surprised and unsuspecting library time looper.

'Eh, who are you?' he answered.

'Never mind that,' said Mr P sternly as he grabbed Mitty by the clothing on his shoulders and dragged him off his normal and well-trodden path.

'Where are we going, stranger?'

'Anywhere but here, dude, you are caught in a monotonous loop and you need to do something different. Or this will be your life forever.'

'I know this already, friend. This is what I have chosen.' Came the immediate response.

Mr P stopped running and instead stopped in the foyer and looked at Mitty face to face. 'Are you saying that you know that you are just repeating everyday over and over again?' asked Mr P.

'Yes. I chose this. I chose this a long time ago. It makes me happy. I have a warm feeling of knowing what's coming; I know I'm safe. And I feel comfortable here. I used to be like you, forever searching for something better but now I don't, and I feel better for it. For me, my friend, life is not about constantly trying for new things or for constant improvement. No, for me life is about simplicity and happiness. And so I traded my house and all my possessions for this and I have never been happier.'

'Wow,' said Mr P. 'I am so sorry, I thought I was saving you, Mitty.'

'You are not the first to say that and you won't be the last. But you are the first to attempt kidnapping I will give you that. Now if you excuse me, kind Dinglewit, I have a staircase to walk up and a stranger to talk to.'

And with that Mitty turned and walked away whistling the tune to the Arabian Derby as he walked.

Now there is a lesson in life thought Mr P. But I don't have the right word for it right now. But he got out his notebook and green crayon and scribbled.

The meaning of life — 9) Be Unprejudiced — not everything is as it seems.

Yeah, that will do for now he thought to himself. And so with the book lodged firmly under his arm he ran towards the exit.

Unfortunately, and this is one thing that Mr P didn't know, was that no book can ever leave the Great library of Angar as it has been forbidden by the Greek God Hermes. And so, as he ran past the detectors there was a sudden whush and a pop and with a puff of smoke the book was gone. Back to its rightful place on the bottom shelf at the very end of the third room in on the right side of the eighth floor.

A place for everything in a universe where entropy will eventually win.

Now rather embarrassed Mr P walked casually out the library doors. No one batted an eyelid.

Cedar's time vortex paradox

You see the big issue with living in a time vortex are
that some things lose their value. For example, there are
no bookmakers on the planet Cedar. This is because
everybody knows the outcome to all events as they are
written down and stored in the library. Well I say
written, it could also waved, magnetised, and even
thought, and stored within the library. In fact all forms
of communication are catered for on the planet Cedar
and their records are kept for all eternity within the
library walls. Every transcribed form of communication
that has ever been recorded, is in there somewhere,
neatly ordered and available for all to see. If you are
famous and wish to know how and when you meet your
maker then simply go to the obituaries and there you
will discover your fate. And there is no changing fate.
On all the other planets and in all the other universes
events will change dependent upon who has a time
machine, but here on Cedar, all the events are recorded
as they eventually happened. If you want to see how the
universe ends then there is a section on that. If you want
to know who wins next year's FA cup final then the
history of the greatest football competition is there in
black and white. And if you really want to know what

happens (or happened) in 3560 then there is a section on that too.

There are no companies that were set up by an entrepreneur, who went on to make billions, because everybody knew about the idea before the entrepreneur had even thought of it, and invested in it themselves, and made a few quid. Nope, here on Cedar the inhabitants live and work as equals purely because there is no other option. Crime is rare because within the library there is a crime database that acts as a deterrent to those wishing to perform a larceny, as every crime is listed before it has happened and the outcome recorded. Marriages and divorces are also listed, but still, it happens — probably because weddings are bloody good fun — although there is a booming trade in pre-nuptial agreements. Within the library walls are fictional novels the likes you wouldn't believe — because they haven't been written yet (trust me you are in for some big surprises). And the floor that concerns itself with music is out of this world, especially when the universe catches up with magno-wave rock.

The biggest loss of value, however, is time. On Cedar time has no value. Everywhere else time is precious; in fact, everywhere else time is the most precious commodity in the universe, but not here. You will never hear the phrase "Time is money" on the planet Cedar. To the locals who have grown up in a time vortex they have no understanding of the value of time. To them, time is just your span of existence on this mortal coil and it cannot be used for profit. In fact, the whole notion of profiteering and making a monetary gain does not enter the brains of Cedarians, who by their own admittance, exist only for fun.

A little bit like Dinglewits.

It was here that Mr P discovered that he was King Arthur of the ancient human Britons but was fascinated as to how that came to be. If he scoured the bookshelves for long enough he would be sure to find out the reason, but to him, time was still very precious and was not prepared to waste any of it looking for trifling nonsense when he had to meaning to life to uncover.

But living in a time vortex does have it advantages. One of which is that you are able to send messages through the dimensions of time to anyone and anywhere in the spectrum of existence. It was to this aim that Mr P decided to write to Geoffrey and tell him of their adventures. Geoffrey always liked a good story being as he was, an avid reader and Mr P wanted to keep in touch in the hope that they would see each other again someday. It wasn't cheap though, forty credits for a thousand English characters and way way way more if you wanted to insert a picture. Mr P opted against this option as he was starting to get a bit skint. And so, with great enthusiasm, he sat and composed a unique letter that he would never have thought possible, and within thirty minutes it was sent, through the ether of time, to Geoffrey, who was living some time in the future.

'What do ya think we should do now, babe?' asked Gertie as they sat on the steps outside the library. They were both at a crossroads with what the next course of action should be.

They both really liked the lifestyle here on Cedar and were wondering was it worth the effort to continue on their journey to the Arushan planets when perhaps they had found their paradise right here.

'A lot of Dinglewits spend their whole lives trying for something better than they have and they never achieve it. They just spend their lives chasing a dream,' Mr P answered, 'I don't wanna be that person!'

'But here we have an opportunity,' Gertie replied, 'no one here seems to realise the importance of hindsight, we know what happens in the future to all the species in all the galaxies and we can warn them and prevent future tragedies from happening.'

'No, we can't, Gertie, the nature of beings is the nature of beings and nothing anyone says will change their mind-set. You know this. All we can do is observe the events from afar and allow nature to take its natural course.'

They both instantly agreed that this is the unfortunate truth and left it at that.

Alchemists and Shamans

At this point in the story, it is probably worth going over the old tale of the King George V penny coins, one of which became known as the liberty coin. Well, these coins were, in fact, keys to time travel with each key enabling travel into a specific point in time. That is except the seventh coin — hereby known as the seventh seal. This was initially placed inside the Holy Grail but unbeknown to anyone was removed by Mr P before Gertie gave the grail to Lancelot in the lake that night. So in fact the seventh seal was actually, and had been all along, in the pocket of Mr P.

Could this be the reason that they had travelled through a time-hole and on to the planet of Cedar? Was the coin such good luck that it prevented them from being eaten by the Goliaths? Was it possible that, like the liberty coin, they were invisible to certain things like the Griffins? Or had the meaning of the seventh seal yet to be revealed?

Ooh it's a mystery…

Sat there on the steps of the library Mr P made a suggestion. 'Let's go and see what this coin is capable of, babe?' he said rather nonchalantly as he pulled the coin out of his pocket.

'Is that what I think it is?' Gertie replied.

'Well, I didn't see the point in leaving it inside the Holy Grail, so I quietly removed it when no one was looking.'

'What do you wanna do with it?'

They both sat and gave it some thought. They both knew that they might have the single greatest object still in existence, seeing as they had already assigned the Holy Grail to the history books, and that they should at least try and have some fun with it.

Gertie agreed. 'Let's go and find a shaman and ask him.'

Now to some "going to find a shaman" may sound like a strange thing to suggest. But with recent events that Mr P and Gertie had experienced it was a perfectly reasonable request.

There are two parts to the city of Angar. There is the new town and the old town. But, unlike the old towns back on Earth, the old town Angar is not a tourist trap, and is not being deliberately kept old to titillate the foreigners. Indeed, old town Angar is like the town that time forgot and is the perfect place to find all the ancient magicians and wizards and sorcerers that are currently roaming the universe looking for mischief. The buildings are all at least a thousand years old and most lean at absurdly funny angles to each other giving the impression that if any one of the buildings was to fall then they would all fall like a set of dominoes. Mr P noticed that every roof was different and made from different materials. There were slate roofs, copper roofs, straw roofs, tiled roofs, and wooden roofs. The copper roofs were Mr P's favourite due to the green tinge that time places on them and when the light changes, then so do they. Mr P had often said that when he finally buys his forever home it would have a copper roof, and hopefully an open fireplace. The cobbled streets appeared to have been set centuries ago and not tended to ever since. But they performed their task well and nobody tripped over the cobbles that protruded above the others.

'Let's try down here, babe,' said Gertie as the pair rambled the endless streets and back alleys. 'There are so many little shops, it's hard to know which one to enter.'

'Aye, and we can't just walk in and ask. We would look a right pair,' replied Mr P before coming to a sudden stop. 'THAT ONE!'

Directly in front on the other side of the street stood a small shop with an old sign saying Alchemist.

'There, Gertie! That's our shop. Let's go look.'

'Really?' replied Gertie while staring at the tatty old shop that obviously nobody visited.

'He is an alchemist, babe. That's just the sort of life form we are looking for.'

They tenuously walked over the busy street and into the cramped, and rather smelly, shop. Which was of course empty. Except for a small man sat in the corner reading a book and smoking a pipe.

'Can I help you?'

'Yes, my name is Mr P and this is Gertie. We were hoping you could help us with this coin we have.' Mr P pulled the coin from his pocket and held it up.

'Yes of course. My name is Jaume.' He got up from his stool and took possession of the coin. 'I haven't seen one of these in a long long time. Quite remarkable. To be honest I am surprised that they still exist and haven't been destroyed. Where did you find it?'

Mr P smiled. 'On a planet called Earth.'

'Of course,' replied Jaume. 'That is where they were made. How many do you have?'

'Just this one.'

'Well, it's one of seven that were made, six of which allow for time travel to a specific moment in time. Do you know what year this coin takes you to?' asked Jaume.

'No idea,' replied Gertie. 'You mentioned six coins. What about the seventh?' she asked.

Jaume turned to face Gertie. 'Well my dear, the seventh coin is very special indeed. It contains powers way beyond anyone's comprehension.'

'What if I was to tell you that this is the seventh coin?' added Mr P.

Jaume looked at the coin 'Then you would have made an old sorcerer very happy indeed. Is this the seventh coin?'

'Yes.'

Jaume passed the coin back to Mr P and said, 'Follow me,' as he led them down a cramped set of stairs to the rear of his shop.

'Do you want to lock your door if we are going downstairs?' asked Gertie.

'Oh, nobody ever comes into this shop,' Jaume replied. 'You are the first customer I have had in months. But please do, you never know.'

Gertie locked the door and quickly joined the others.

As they entered the cellar they were immediately greeted with a sea of warm light. And books. So many books.

'Please take a stool. Would you like some tea?'

'Yes please,' answered Mr P. 'Do you have apple tea?'

'Of course, every sorcerer has apple tea.' And he began to pour water into some old dusty goblets.

'This coin is powerful,' Jaume added as he passed over the goblets. 'I've seen it before, you need to be careful what you do with it.'

'Where were they made?' asked Gertie.

'Well, the coins themselves were minted on Earth by some king or other, but the actual magical ingredient is still a mystery,' Jaume answered. 'What do you know about ancient human alchemy?'

'Not much,' answered Gertie.

'Have you heard of Ayahuasca? asked Jaume.

'No.'

'What about the writings of Eirenaeus Philalethes?' Jaume endeavoured.

'No.'

'The Hartlib Circle?'

'No.'

'The Invisible College?'

'No.'

'What about Comenius and the Pansophic Principle?'

'No. Sorry.'

Jaume looked forlorn. 'We have a lot to discuss tonight then,' he added. 'I presume you have heard of Nostradamus?'

'Yes,' chipped in Mr P, 'we *have* heard of him, he is well famous.'

'Well, that's a start then, so how many of *my* poems?'

This took Mr P and Gertie by surprise and they both sat speechless for a few seconds. 'Are you Nostradamus?' asked Gertie.

'Well, my surname is Nostradamus but the person you know is my brother Michel. But the poems that you know of are *my* work,' he said pointing at his chest, 'fat load of good they did though. I sometimes wish I hadn't bothered. Nobody listened to a bloody word we said.'

'You mean, you wrote all those prophecies?' asked Mr P. 'Why?'

'To try and warn everybody, but nobody listens. They never do. I've written thousands over the years in every language and to every species, but nobody listens. I guess it's just the nature of things,' Juame continued.

'We were thinking of doing the same thing,' added Mr P. 'The problem with your work is your clues are too cryptic. Nobody really understands them until after the event. Then they get used as a sort of hindsight. Rather than a useful tool for the future.'

'They have to be cryptic you see, to get past the council of censorship. You see the council don't want to interfere in the events of the universe. They believe that it's bad for the overall balance. So all messages have to be cryptic in order to be accepted. They were my fourth submission, and even then, they only scraped through by one vote.'

'Oh, so that's it then?' stated Gertie. 'We can't prevent the Orion wars or any of the other disasters? We have to sit back and let it all happen?'

'I'm afraid so,' answered Juame. 'It is a privilege to live here on Cedar, but that is the burden that you must carry.'

'Well, that's a bit shit,' Mr P interjected.

Juame looked at Mr P in a sympathetic tone. He was once where Mr P 'Yes, it is. But you can't do everything. All you can do is have an influence on the small dimension that is your life, and let everyone else get on with theirs.'

A silence gripped the room for about two seconds. Until… BANG BANG on the front door of the shop.

'That's not good,' said Juame, 'no one ever comes to my shop, and the day that the seventh seal appears here I have banging at the door.'

A look of concern happened about the face of the old and distinguished shop owner. 'You should all hide, it isn't safe here for you,' he continued. 'Who are they?' asked Mr P.

'Well, my guess would be home-time security. They must know of your presence here. And more accurately the presence of the coin.'

Juame scurried into the corner of the cellar and opened the door of an old cupboard. 'Quickly hide in here.'

'What it's just an old cupboard. They will find us in there,' answered Gertie.

'No, they won't. It's a matter distorter. It will transport you over to the telephone booth across the road. This is my escape route should this ever happen. Quick get in.' Mr P and Gertie struggled into the cupboard and Juame gently shut the door. Just at that time there was a huge bang upstairs as the front door of the shop had been kicked in, followed by the clambering of footsteps down the cramped staircase. For Mr P and Gertie the light from the room vanished and was replaced by the daylight of being outside again. Juame was right; they were outside in the phone booth.

'Let's make a run for it, Gertie. This way.'

'What about Juame?' Gertie replied.

'He should be safe without us there, babe. It's us they are after.'

'Oh, I do hope so,' she replied.

And with that they were both running down the cobbled street.

'There they are,' came the cries from the security team as they left the shop after figuring out that they had been duped.

Mr P took Gertie's hand and quickly changed direction and ran into a nearby shop and continued up the stairs to the top floor. Behind them they could hear their chasers enter the shop.

'WHERE DID THEY GO?'

And the sound of footsteps clambering up a flight of stairs followed.

Mr P and Gertie got to the top of the shop and exited the shop onto a flat roofed patio. It was full of flowerpots. They stopped and looked around in all directions.

'Babe, this way. There is a bridge leading to another building.'

They immediately ran across the poorly built bridge as dust came up from its wooden floorboards as they ran across.

On the other side of the bridge was a patio with more flowerpots. 'Jeez they like their flowers here, Gertie.'

'Yes, very pretty, babe. But we can come back another time and marvel in their beauty, eh.'

'Of course, Yeah. Look there's a door.'

As they approached the door to another shop, and seemingly a route to safety, the glass window that provided some sunshine to the otherwise dull looking door exploded.

They both ducked down and looked back to find three brutish looking cycloptic life forms with big guns in their hands heading towards them. They tried to stand up but were immediately forced back down by more shots from their lazer guns.

'Babe, what shall we do?' asked Gertie in a desperate voice. 'I dunno, Gertie, perhaps we should surrender.'

'What about the coin? Can that help us?'

Mr P grabbed Gertie's hand and with his other hand held the coin. 'Err... Oh magical coin... err... transport us toooo... that roof over there,' said Mr P. And in a puff of smoke, they were immediately transported.

'Woohoo,' they both shouted in unison as they saw the armed Cyclops's approach their previous position and wonder where they had gone.

'This coin, Gertie. This coin is magic. Wey-hey we have a magic coin,' whispered Mr P.

'No wonder they are after it, babe,' Gertie replied, 'but how did they know how to find us?'

'I dunno, maybe it has some sort effect on the time vortex here, or they were tipped off, or maybe it was written in the library and they were waiting for us. Oh, I dunno.'

'It can't have been written in the library otherwise they would have known that we transported here and they will have security here waiting for us,' Gertie replied.

They both lay there motionless waiting for some security guards to happen upon them with laser guns at the ready. But nothing. They continued to look around. But no one came. After treating themselves to a quick peep across to the other rooftop they gingerly made their way down an external fire escape and onto the cobbled streets below.

'Right, babe,' said Mr P, 'don't look suspicious. We should head back to the ship and get out of here.'

'Good plan.'

They put their arms around each other and walked quickly back through the crowded streets while hugging the inside of the buildings as they went.

They walked over Watlin Street and up through a tight passage that led to the river. From there they turned left and headed towards the great fountain of Pain which, in its heyday would have looked tremendous, but now is an old decaying brick water feature that should have been replaced a while ago.

'Is that Juame?' asked Gertie as they approached the fountain. Juame was stood, looking in all directions, like he knew that they would be in that general vicinity but not quite sure where.

'Yeah, it's him. How did he know where to come?' answered Mr P. 'It looks safe let's go see.'

'Can we trust him?'

'We have no choice, babe.'

They approached Juame quite nervously as they were not sure whether he was the one who tipped them off. But being trusting souls who considered themselves a good judge of character they decided to make contact.

'Oh, there you are,' shouted Juame as he saw the two nervous Dinglewits approach him. 'I thought they would find you.'

'How did you know we would be here?' asked Gertie.

'I didn't,' came the answer, 'but this is the crossroads to the city so it was as good a place as any to bump into you. Come we must get to safety and away from the surveillance cameras because that must be how they found you.'

He positioned himself into the middle of our two time-travelling heroes and put his arms around both. 'Come this way,' he said.

'How come they found us?' asked Gertie.

'Well although you are invisible to cameras and surveillance equipment you sort of cause a distortion in them as you walk. This can be detected, AND they are looking for you,' Juame answered. 'My car is over there.'

They got into Juame's old clapped-out motor vehicle , and with smoke bellowing from the exhaust pipe, trundled down the cobbled streets.

After a few turns, and stops at traffic lights, they eventually left the hustle and bustle of the city and into the suburbs. This was totally different form the busy streets and roads that they had become accustomed. The roads are still cobbled, as seemed to the way here, but instead of countless motor vehicles there are mini elephants pulling carts, and vast variety of life forms carrying groceries and livestock.

Juame pulled over into an off-road diner. 'You guys, OK?' he asked caringly.

'Yes, we are good ta,' answered Gertie.

'OK then! Now, about this coin. What can it do?' asked Mr P.

'Ah yes, the coin,' answered Juame. 'Well, it's a magical insouciant coin you see.'

'OOH,' said Mr P and Gertie in sync together. They then looked at each other and laughed.

'Well,' continued Juame, 'the person that carries the coin has a feeling of being carefree and un-troubled, as well as possessing magical powers. That's why it is always kept with the Holy Grail. In fact, to me it's the most valuable of all the coins.'

'How so?' asked Gertie.

'Because life is all about enjoying yourself, being happy. If you are happy then everything else falls into place.'

'Juame!' said Mr P. 'You have wisdom beyond your years.'

And with that he pulled out his notebook and green crayon and wrote.

The meaning of life — 10) Enjoy life.

He put away his notebook and swiftly said to Juame, 'My friend. Take us back to our ship if you don't mind. We have planets to be.' And with those immortal words they left the planet Cedar, never to return.

Geoffrey

Geoffrey was a Dinglewit that loved to read. He would sit for days upon end reading anything that he could get his hands on. At school, he would often be in trouble for not doing his homework because he started reading a book, and just forgot about all his other work. Books are his life. He was a native Welsh man that moved to the middle lands of Britannia when he was a child and met up with Mr P and Cleese to form the original LPMD. Whenever the three were together, trouble was never far behind.

This was the Geoffrey who, on a cold dank night in December, received a message from his good friend Mr P explaining recent adventures from inside the wormhole. Geoffrey loved it and thought 'Hey, this is a great idea for a book.' And with that he sat down at his table and began scribing. Now Geoffrey was the sort of Dinglewit that never liked to confuse a good story with the truth, and so with some garnishing, the book was finished. And thus, the story of King Arthur and his Knights of the Round Table entered the literature for all to read.

Now this is quite good Geoffrey thought to himself I'm gonna try and send it to Mr P to see what he thinks.

Now the method by which he was going to achieve this was simple. He had received a message through the universal ether and was simply going to attach a document to the message and press "Reply".

Yep, that'll do it he thought and he pressed "Reply".

Now the only problem with this is that messages into, and out of, Cedar are read by the administrators and can, sometimes, get muddled up let's say. And unfortunately, that is what happened here. The story itself passed through the hands of the administrators without any problems at all — no issues there. The big problem was the year. It is still not known how it happened but the year of writing was catalogued as 1138 AD human time. And so as soon as Geoffrey tried to get his book published it was quickly pointed out to him that the story had already been written. OOPS.

But this begs the question of fate.

As Geoffrey wrote his story based loosely on a message received from a time vortex, how was it that it came true? Are our lives loosely mapped out or can we completely make our own world?

Paradise found

The search for paradise had had a positive effect on Mr P and Gertie. They spent more time together than ever before, and they soon realised how much they actually enjoyed each other's company. This is something they had forgotten while on the twists and turns of everyday life back on Earth. Mr P remembered how funny Gertie could be with her quick-witted humour and bad jokes, and conversely, Gertie began to appreciate the warmth and compassion that Mr P offers — aside from his masculinity that is. So it could be said that while on their journey to find paradise, they also discovered the love that they had for each other.

That said, the arrival on the Arushan planet of Lopoe had put them right back in the firing line.

Lopoe was akin to paradise. The waterfalls were as majestic as can be seen anywhere in the universe, and the mountains are a view that are rarely seen except to avid mountaineers.

They landed on a deserted plain just outside of a small village called Manaclan, a quaint little dwelling comprised of wooden wigwams and igloo shaped houses. From a distance all that can be seen are the plumes of smoke coming from the many open fires, and the blossom trees that line the outer edge of the village.

The main path into the village was a well-trodden dirt track that had the feel of centuries of use. Lopoe didn't have cities, and only had a couple of towns for that matter, as they believed that the fresh open air is good for the soul and everyone has a right to it. The many villages and holts in the region worked together to form communities, where every need was tended, and where everyone looked out for everyone else. All appeared well.

'Idyllic,' said Mr P as he, Gertie, Mya, and Boomer walked towards the village, 'I feel at home here.'

'Me too,' replied Gertie. 'And me,' chipped in Mya.

'Well, I hope they like us then,' Mr P continued.

And they made their way towards the wooden structure that looked like the gateway to the village.

It was a lovely spring morning.

As they approached the gatehouse a voice shouted 'HALT. WHO GOES THERE?'

Now this was a turn up for the old plus fours, thought Mr P. This is supposed to be paradise and yet, here they are, the villagers, defending themselves with barriers and guards.

'Err… It's Mr P and my family from Earth. Err… We come in peace.' He smiled in satisfaction and looked at Gertie.

'We come in peace? Why say that?' asked Gertie.

'Dunno, babe. I just heard that that is what you are supposed to say, in these sorts of circumstances.'

'WAIT THERE,' came the response from the gatehouse. And for a few minutes there seemed to be no activity whatsoever.

'Shall we just leave?']asked Gertie.

'Umm… Probably… I dunno,' replied Mr P.

Just then the wooden gates opened and a squat little dwarf proudly walked out to greet them. 'What ya want?' came the introduction.

'Umm… I dunno… We have travelled here from Earth to find paradise,' Mr P responded.

There was a brief pause. 'Follow me then!' came the confident response from the dwarf. And he turned and walked back into the village. They followed him.

'Welcome to Manaclan Village,' he continued. 'Pub,' pointing to an old looking tavern.

'Food,' pointing with the other hand to an open stall.

Inside the gates the settlement was divine. The whole of the village was awash with bright coloured flowers, children playing, and groups of different life forms laughing and joking with each other. Mostly, however, the village was full of dwarfs.

'This is lovely,' added Gertie, 'is there anywhere to sleep?'

'There,' said the dwarf pointing to a pyramid shaped wooden structure. He then walked off.

'Huh. Err OK. Let's go there then,' Mr P chipped in.

They walked towards the pyramid with a feeling that this could quite easily be their new home.

They entered the pyramid and were greeted by the village elder, dressed in bright gowns, and wearing a hat that is slightly too big for him.

'Welcome, Earthlings. My name is Vigo,' he said, bowing quite reservedly. 'I'm afraid you find us in hard times.'

Mr P turned to face the dwarf mayor, 'I'm sorry, sir, but is it possible to speak slower. We are new here and you seem to speak very fast indeed?'

'Of course,' came the response in a tone eager to please. 'My name is Vigo, I am the elder in this village. I'm afraid you find us in hard times. We are expecting an invasion of hostile forces.'

'Oh god really, I'm so sorry to hear that,' answered Gertie.

'Yes, we have been invaded by the Empire. There is to be a battle. Very soon I suspect.'

'That is terrible,' added Mr P.

'Hopefully the villages will come together otherwise we are all doomed.'

Gertie snuggled in to Mr P, and put her arms tightly around his waist. 'Vigo,' she muttered. 'I am so sorry that this is happening to you. This seems like a peaceful place, and everybody is happy here.'

'It is a peaceful place, my dear,' answered Vigo, 'all the villages around here are peaceful. Over the centuries we have built ourselves a little piece of paradise. That is why we must defend it.'

'Well, I will help you!' called out Mr P.

This got a response from Gertie. 'Babe! What are you saying?' she whispered. 'Why don't we just leave?'

'Because some things are worth protecting, Gertie. I want a paradise for us. And if we have to defend it then so be it. This feels right, babe.'

Gertie felt the same too and took Mr P by the hand. 'Then I am by your side, babe,' she responded. 'So let's bring the Pretty Flamingo inside, find a place to live, and get some food.'

Boomer barked in agreement.

The next few days passed peacefully, they had, indeed, found their paradise. They became very good friends with a lot of the village dwarves, who looked up to them (oops). Mya had made some new friends too. And even Boomer had become romantically attached.

Mr P had been holding meetings with elders from the neighbouring villages and they had come to an agreement that they would all stick together should the Empire invade. Due to his size and enthusiasm, Mr P was looked upon as the overall leader and was asked to come up with a warrior name for which he should be addressed. Naturally he chose the title of Arthur.

And from that day on Mr P would be known as Arthur. He liked that. It felt like fate.

The Battle of Manaclan

And it was on one grey morning did fate finally play its role.

Mr P was lying in bed cuddling Gertie, and looking up at the bright morning sky, when the sound of bells rang out.

'There here… there here…' came the screams from guards at the gatehouse. Mr P quickly got out of his bed and looked out of the window. In the distance was the dust from an advancing army.

'They are here, babe.'

Gertie jumped out of bed. 'What shall we do?'

'Grab Mya and Boomer and get into The Pretty Flamingo. I need to know you're all gonna be safe. And should we lose the battle… Leave. And take Vigo's family with you.'

Gertie did not like this at all, but she understood that Mr P had to do this.

He kissed her for one final time, put on his helmet, grabbed the magical coin and his sword, and walked out through the wooden gates to lead the villagers from the front. Gertie did exactly what they agreed, and watched the upcoming battle from the Pretty Flamingo cuddled up next to Mya and Boomer.

As Mr P walked to the front of the gathering villagers cries of ARTHUR, ARTHUR, rang out. And as the passing moments fell more and more dwarves from the neighbouring villagers swelled the ranks of the defending force.

Slowly the invaders approached. The dust clouds from their boots grew bigger. The villagers were ready, standing side by side with their shields in front, and their swords at the ready. The banging of the invader drums got louder, and the grip on the defenders' swords got tighter.

Within minutes the Empire invaders were within 200 metres. They had more soldiers — but not by much — but these were hardened warriors. The villagers on the other hand were a rag tag bunch of farmers and clothes makers. But they were defending their homes and their families.

Vigo and the elders from the villagers joined Mr P at the front and asked, 'Arthur. What shall we do?'

Mr P took his sword in his right hand and held the coin in his left. He turned to his new friends and held his sword aloft.

Vigo followed suit, as did the elders of the other villages.

'I am Arthur. Follow me and defeat this great enemy of ours. Are you with me?'

'YEEEEEEEAH!' came the shrieks from the villagers.

And with one final look into the heavens Mr P took a few steps forwards and shouted, 'CHAAAAARGE.'

The villagers ran forward in an un-corrupted line eager to make contact with the Empire invaders.

The noise and the adrenaline reached fever pitch. Behind the running lines were the drummers, beating their drums in synchronicity, willing on the defending heroes. Arthur led from the front.

The faces of the invaders grew bigger, and the adrenaline pumped through his body. He once wrote in his notebook that a meaning to life is to live a little dangerously — but this was taking that to the extreme he thought. Still, it's too late to turn back now. The invading line got ever closer.

The defending villagers ran ever faster.

'Arthur, Arthur, we won't break through that line it's impenetrable,' shouted Vigo, over the noise of the running villagers.

Arthur looked along the line of the Empire soldiers and could not see an obvious weak point. All along the line were shields with pikes and spears facing forward. Awaiting the kill of an advancing dwarf.

Arthur knew that Vigo was right. He needed to do something, and do it now before all was lost.

He hoped that the magical powers of the seventh seal did not betray him now.

He grasped the coin ever tighter in his hand and shouted. 'HEAVENS ABOVE, LET LIGHTNING STRIKE THESE FOES OF FREEDOM!'

Suddenly, the heavens opened up, and a dozen bolts of lightning lit up the battlefield decimating the line of invaders. Arthur looked left and right and saw many dozens of the Empire's finest warriors catapulted high into the air in an explosive plume. This made holes in the invaders' line, and so, with an almighty CRASH, Arthur, Vigo and the villagers ploughed into the attacking line.

Immediately the screams of battle could be heard. And this was close combat battle.

Seeing an enemy directly in front Arthur swung his sword and with an amazing THUD it took down an Empire fighter. Blood seeped through the helmet of the dying invader, and Arthur noticed the life ooze from his body.

But there was no time to dwell. From his left came a swing from a jagged edged sword, and Arthur had to duck before it took his head off at the neck. He temporarily lost his footing in the mud but quickly manoeuvred to a kneeling position.

Now on one knee, he lunged his sword forward into the stomach of an invader, who immediately fell to the ground with both hands holding his intestines in place.

He looked around to see individual battles everywhere. In some places the village dwarves lay dead on the floor in other places the invaders were dead. He looked at his own sword and noticed the trickle of blood down the shaft.

Just then there was an almighty yell. 'YAAAAA,' it was an Empire fighter with an axe held high above his head, and about to strike down Arthur where he knelt. He quickly rolled over to the left and with a back arm swing cut down the attacker. Directly to his right Arthur noticed his new friend, Ludo, in the throes of death, but could do nothing to help him. In fact, he noticed that a large number of dwarves were laid dead in that small region of mud. There was obviously something deadly nearby. He looked behind and saw a sabre toothed Rhinosaw wreaking havoc. He was not able to kill the beast with his own sword, but something needed to be done, and done quickly. So he grasped the coin once more and called upon its powers. 'FIRE AND DEATH TO THE BEAST,' he yelled.

In an instant the Rhinosaw burst into flames, and let out an almighty roar, as it fell to the ground. He looked around for more but everywhere he looked all he could see were soldiers in the midst of fighting for their lives. He took a deep breath, but out of the corner of his eye he could see Vigo in trouble. He immediately got up from his fighting position and ran to help his new friend. Vigo was laid on his back helpless and was about to be killed when suddenly, CRUNCH! Arthur's sword entered through the back of the invader and came out of the front. Arthur quickly pulled it out and helped VIGO off the floor. 'There you go, old chap. You live to fight another day.'

'Thank you, Arthur,' replied Vigo.

Arthur looked around the battlefield. It was too close to call. They noticed that the generals of the Empire were in a group at the top of the hill surrounded by royal guards to keep them safe. The guards were dressed in a long red robe that partially hid their metal armour. From their vantage point the generals were dictating the tactics of the battle, and were directing troops to the weak spots within the dwarf ranks. And they were doing a good job too. Arthur and Vigo both knew that if the battle carried on as it was, then the day would be lost.

Then in an instant they noticed a large group of invaders heading straight towards them. Obviously, the generals had seen Arthur's handiwork and were taking action. 'Do something, Arthur!' Vigo yelled.

Arthur looked up to the sky. There were so many of them. Surely, they were doomed. With nothing to lose he grasped firmly on the coin once more and shouted, 'FIRE AND BRIMSTONE BE MY WEAPON. I COMMAND THEE.'

He pointed his sword at the hordes of invading soldiers and unleashed an unstoppable line on fire. 'ARGGGGGH!' came the cries from the villainous Empire warriors as they caught fire and began rolling around on the floor in an attempt to immerse themselves in mud. Other soldiers immediately turned to dust and blew away in the wind.

This created some breathing space for the exhausted defending dwarves, but they still took time to cheer and dance as they saw their foes disintegrate into ashes.

Vigo picked up a spear that was lying on the floor and threw it at one of the generals. 'Get them,' he called to Arthur.

Arthur looked up at the generals, who were surrounded by their personal guards and watching the action from afar, and thought if we get them then the rest will desert.

'You're right, Vigo. Leave it to me.'

He gripped the coin once more. 'GOLLIATHS OF THE UNIVERSE — JOIN ME,' he shouted.

The skies darkened and a beam of light suddenly appeared. All the fighting warriors stopped for a second and looked up.

The shadow of wings could be seen at first, followed by the rest of the Goliath's body.

Arthur held up his sword and pointed directly at the Goliaths. And then with a sudden movement pointed at the generals perched at the top of the hill.

'ATTACK!' he shouted, and in one momentous action, the Goliaths flew over the fractured lines of fighters and straight towards the generals.

'Woohoor,' came the shouts of joy from the village dwarves as the Goliaths flew overhead and straight at the dastardly Empire scoundrels.

CHOMP CHOMP, CRUNCH CRUNCH, came the noise, over the top of loud screams, as the Goliaths began biting and eating the invading generals, and their guards.

A few started to retreat, then a few more, then within seconds the entire invading force had turned around and were now running back towards their boats. Followed VERY closely by the hungry Goliaths that were determined to fill their stomachs as much as possible.

'After them!' shouted Vigo while holding up his sabre.

And in one fell swoop the entire dwarf army chased down the Empire rats and killed as many as they could.

Arthur, now extremely tired, mustered up one last effort and joined in the rout. He knew this was nasty business. But it was necessary business if there was to be peace in paradise.

They ran and they ran. Chopping down the attacking rogues as they made their way back to the invading vessels. Blood filled the grass plains, and the little stream that meandered wilfully through the vines had a temporary red tinge to it.

The few invaders that made it back to their boats quickly gave sail and left — vowing never to return.

They were victorious. They had come together and defeated the enemy. Their lives and the lives of those they love were saved. Paradise was preserved. And peace was finally achieved.

Mr P stood on the banks of the river watching the invaders sail back home with their tails between their legs. He suddenly had a thought. 'The story of King Arthur had come true. He had united a kingdom and defended them against an invading army. Was he truly King Arthur?

He walked slowly back to village. In his path was a panorama of death and destruction where wild flowers would normally grow. He knew that the hardship and destruction would have been greater had they not fought, but that was skank consolation right now.

He looked up at Gertie who was restlessly watching the returning soldiers, and who gleamed when she saw him.

They ran to each other and hugged. Really, really, tightly. 'I need a drink, beautiful,' Mr P said.

'Me too, babe, let's get drunk!' Gertie answered. Vigo and the village dwarves of Manaclan joined them. And they all got drunk together.

The meaning of life

The following months passed, and peace was restored to the villages. In fact, the Empire cancelled the invasion of Lopoe forever and signed a peace treaty. Life in paradise was now complete.

One morning, while nursing a sore head, Mr P sat on the porch of his new and beloved home and reached for his notebook. He flicked through the pages where he had written his notes — in green crayon of course — to see whether he had discovered the meaning to life.

'I feel self-actualised, my darling,' said Mr P to Gertie as they sat on the couch. 'I think this is the happiest and most content I have ever been.'

'Me too, let's stay here,' she replied.

'I've been looking through my notebook and this is what I had written down,' Mr P continued.

The Meaning of Life

The meaning of life — 1) Be inquisitive
The meaning of life — 2) Be adventurous
The meaning of life — 3) Be magical
The meaning of life — 4) Be Nice
The meaning of life — 5) Be open-minded

The meaning of life — 6) Live a little dangerously

The meaning of life — 7) Be authentic

The meaning of life — 8) Improve your world.

The meaning of life — 9) Be Unprejudiced — not everything is as it seems

The meaning of life — 10) Enjoy life

'What do you think? Have I unmasked the meaning to life?' he asked

'Well, it's possible that you've unmasked the meaning to your life. But everyone is different you see,' she answered.

'Hmm. I hadn't thought of that. But then I suppose everyone's life is different and it's just important to find meaning to your own life.' He continued, 'Well to me I think these ten things are the meaning to my life, I have written them down. Let me tell you what they are.'

Gertie knew that there was no way out of this, so she got comfy in her seat and bedded in for the long haul.

'Well,' began Mr P, 'first of all one needs to be inquisitive. It's important to question one's own situation in order to learn new things. Don't you think, Gertie?'

'Oh yes absolutely.'

'Yes, quite correct,' continued Mr P 'So that is meaning number one. Number two is to be adventurous. Do you remember our quiet life before we began this adventure, babe? And how much we have changed because of the journey we took. Goodness it seems like another lifetime ago now.'

Gertie smiled at Mr P and placed her head on a comfy pillow.

'Number three. Be magical, Gertie. Life is way too short to just blend in and exist. One needs to glow and brighten the room as they walk in don't you think? I do. Number four is to be nice. It's important to be nice. If you are not nice then you are not worthy of existence.'

Now that was something Gertie could agree with. The first thing she noticed when first meeting Mr P was how nice he was. She liked nice.

'Number five, Gertie, is to be open-minded. I learnt that when we met Frisby. Do you remember Frisby, babe? I do hope he found what he was looking for you know. Number six is to live dangerously. Well, we have certainly done that, and it makes you appreciate life. And number seven is to be authentic. Yes, be yourself and no one else. That is important.'

Gertie leaned over and picked up her drink. This is going to take a while and so she will need hydration.

'I put improve your world as number eight Gertie. What I mean by that is to make the world a better place for you having been on it. And number nine is to be unprejudiced. Yes, yes, good old Mitty. Hmm happily living his best life in the library and not seeing the need to make things any more complicated than they are. He found his happiness there.'

Gertie chipped in. 'I never met Mitty. Where did you meet him?'

'I met him in the great library. He voluntarily put himself in a time loop. Intriguing situation that I would like to have more time to explore. But hey-ho, on to number ten, and probably the most important of all. Enjoy life. I think we sometimes forget how short life can be, and how important it is to enjoy it.'

'Amen to that,' said Gertie.

'So what do you think, Gertie? Have I cracked the meaning to life?'

'Well, they all sound plausible to me, you should make up a poem or a fable or something,' she replied.

This seemed like an excellent idea to Mr P. If only he could think of something catchy, then that would complete the journey. They are living in paradise and have been on this fantastic voyage of discovery. It seems only right to finish it with something catchy.

For the next few days, he tinkered around with verses and rhymes but nothing stuck. He drafted a story but that was too long winded and he wanted something punchier. So one night, while sat in the bath, he decided to write the first letters of each word to see if he could come up with something.

I.A.M.N.O.D.A.I.U.E.

IAM... 'No that wouldn't work.'

DEMON... 'No that wouldn't work either.'

And then there it was. The very word that describes the meaning to life. EUDAIMONIA

'Yes,' shouted Mr P, like it was his Eureka moment. 'Eudaimonia eudaimonia. That is the meaning to life. Eudaimonia…'

He smiled and leaned back into his bath.

He had come to the end of this journey.

'I think I'll make it into a badge,' he said.

He then put the green crayon and notepad on the wooden stool, that was situated to the side of the bath, and washed his beard.

Eudaimonia

The meaning of life will be different for every different living species. A flower, for example, lives only to pollinate the next generation of flower and to ensure that the basic instinct of survival continues. The capsaicin levels of chilli peppers have evolved alongside the fast metabolism of birds to spread their seeds, and have used that symbiotic relationship to maintain their survival. Further up the food chain butterflies have a genetic deposition to seek out a particular part of the Earth that can sometimes take three generations to achieve.

In fact, when you consider a meaning to existence, it is nigh on impossible to pin it down to anything other than simplistic needs. And that is the need to exist in as much comfort as possible, and to ensure the survival of the species. This is evidenced in sea squirts, who dissolve their own brains once they have found an appropriate rock. And in certain male spiders that are eaten once they have mated in order to provide protein for their offspring.

In low complex life forms, nature has an obvious answer to its actions and can be easily explained. But where the central nervous systems are complex, things get a little more complicated. Hierarchy and selfish genes come into play.

Dinglewits, as with humans, not only wish to exist and reproduce, but they also demand happiness, wealth, a sense of worth, and much more besides. This makes meaning an individual property and not one single generic sentence.

Except for this one.

There is no meaning unique to a species; meaning is unique to the individual.

EUDAIMONIA…

THE END